COMEDY OF THE DEAD

ANTHONY GIANGREGORIO

**NOW AVAILABLE
FROM
UNDEAD PRESS**

ZOMBIE TALES
HOUSE OF TERRORS
THE FALL OF PITTSBURGH: A ZOMBIE NOVEL
DEADLY HUNT: A ZOMBIE SURVIVAL STORY
THE DAY THE WORLD DIED: A ZOMBIE STORY
ZOMBIE KILL: PREDATOR OR PREY?
VICTORY OF THE DEAD: A ZOMBIE STORY
AN UNDEAD CHRISTMAS: A ZOMBIE ANTHOLOGY
ZOMBIES AND FAIRY TALES: AN UNDEAD ANTHOLOGY

Copyright © 2014 Anthony Giangregorio
ISBN Softcover ISBN 13: 978-1-61199-084-3 ISBN 10: 1-611990-84-X
All rights reserved.
Undead Press is an imprint of Living Dead Press. www.livingdeadpress.com
No part of this book may be reproduced or transmitted in any form or by
any means, electronic or mechanical, including photocopying, recording, or
by any information storage and retrieval system, without permission in
writing from the copyright owner.
This is a work of fiction.
Names, characters, places and incidents either are the product of the author's
imagination or are used fictitiously, and any resemblance to any actual
persons, living or dead, events, or locales is entirely coincidental.
This book was printed in the United States of America.
For more info on obtaining additional copies of this book, go to:
www.undeadpress.com
Cover art by Jason Mooers

com·e·dy (kŏm´ĭ-dē)

n. pl. com·e·dies

1. A dramatic work that is light and often humorous
or satirical in tone and that usually contains a happy
resolution of the thematic conflict.

2. A humorous element of life or literature.

3. A humorous occurrence.

Chapter 1

Sleeping fitfully on the floor of the television studio, Pam Patterson shook her head back and forth in the throws of a nightmare. But then she was pulled from the dream by the sound of someone farting, long and loud, right in her face.

She snapped open her eyes to see an ass there, no more than an inch from her nose. The owner of the ass hadn't showered in days, much like Pam, and the rankness of said ass was overpowering. If you then added in the aroma of digested burrito, what you got was a stinkiness not to be improved by mankind for a long time.

For just a few more seconds Pam sat there, breathing in the horrible scent, then she pushed up and rose to her feet, shoving the owner of the ass out of her way.

"What the hell, Pam?" the owner of the ass snapped. He was the copyboy for the studio, a young man no more than nineteen with pimples and thick glasses. No doubt in school he'd gotten his ass kicked every day and the odds that he'd been laid either in school or after was even more doubtful. Pam didn't care for him much. She knew his name was Richard, but other than that she didn't know or care. He was an asshole, really, and the only reason he had the job was because his uncle owned the TV station.

"What the hell indeed," Pam replied, snapping equally as much. "You just farted in my face."

"How do you know it was me?" he asked. "There's a lot of people inside this control booth."

"What did you have for lunch today?" she asked.

"Burritos, why?"

"Yeah, it was you."

Richard sighed. "Okay, you got me. I farted."

"No shit." She slugged him on the arm and he grimaced, then rubbed the limb and moved away from her. Pam wiped her eyes as she took in her surroundings. The studio was buzzing with activity, everyone looking like shit. It had been days since any of them had had any real rest. To say it was a fucked up situation would have been an understatement.

Pam left the booth and went over to the far corner of the studio and got a cup of coffee from the small table there. She took a long sip and then spit out the cold, stale liquid, while yelling, "Jesus, this taste like shit!"

"Oh," someone called from nearby. "So does that mean you've eaten shit before? Was it creamy or chunky?"

"Fuck you, asshole!" she yelled back, not even knowing who had said it. For all she knew, it was the President of the Untied States. She didn't care. She was exhausted and wanted a shower desperately. And her pussy itched like a motherfucker. No one's pussy should itch the way hers did. At the end of the day, washing in the studio's bathroom sink just didn't cut it. She glanced over her shoulder to see if anyone was watching her, and when she thought she was safe, she turned to the side and scratched her coochie.

"Hey, Pam's playing with herself," a voice yelled from her side.

Shit, she hadn't see Roy over there dealing with the lights.

"Shut the fuck up, Roy, and do your job," she snapped.

Roy raised his hand to his mouth, made two fingers into a V, and slid his tongue between them, wiggling it back and forth.

"Pig. In your dreams." Pam made a disgusted face and flipped Roy off, who laughed long and loud before returning to work.

Pam turned to look at the show being broadcast right now. The newsroom desk was set up and two men were sitting behind it, arguing vehemently.

"Look, asshole," the first man yelled, a newsman who had lost all sense of decorum since the dead began to walk. "No one gives two shits why the dead are walking. They're fucking walking! That's what matters. On my way here I saw an old woman who was trying to get her cat out of a tree. I saw her surrounded and taken down by a mob of those things. They ate her face off, tore her chest open. It was un-fucking believable!"

"Why didn't you help her?" the second man asked. He had the typical look of a scientist; a book-smart guy who knew nothing of the real world, academia being his world. He had a scruffy beard, was balding on top and wore thin, wire-rimmed spectacles.

"Help who?" the anchorman asked.

"The old woman, you just told me you saw her murdered before your eyes, yet you did nothing."

The anchorman looked taken aback. "Of course I did nothing. What do I look like, the fucking police? I'm not risking my ass for some old crone."

"And that's exactly the problem, sir," the scientist said, his tone one of superiority. "We all must pull together here, must fight these abominations as one group. But like every disaster that's come before, it's every man for himself."

"Hell yeah, it's every man for himself!" the anchorman said and looked out past the bright lights to the studio crew. "Am I right, guys?"

"Yeah," one man said.

"You're right, Bill," another said.

"Fucking A," came from yet another of the crew.

The scientist was growing angry, but he fought down his urge to yell, knowing it would accomplish nothing. Deep down within him, he had a mental image of putting a gun to the anchorman's head and squeezing the trigger, and blowing the asshole's brains all over the desk they sat behind. He had to accept that the anchorman, like so many others, were simply people who couldn't understand the greater picture.

Pam went back to the control room, where two men were sitting behind a bank of dials and switches. To the side of the man on Pam's far right was a Penthouse magazine. Pam made another disgusted face, something she did a lot. She wasn't the happiest person on a normal day and the dead walking hadn't made her disposition any better.

"Tom, get that filthy magazine out of this control booth right now," she snapped.

Tom lowered the headphones from his ears and looked over at Pam, who was standing there with her arms crossed over her small but pert breasts.

Tom picked up the magazine, holding it near him. "You mean this magazine?"

"Yes," she said. "*That* magazine. It's disgusting. I want it out of here right now."

Tom grinned as he looked at the other man, a bearded guy named George. "But then how would I get to see women with decent-sized tits and ones that didn't have a stick up their ass?"

"Oooooooh, oh no he didn't," George said, waving his hand before him and swaying his head back and forth like an old black woman would do.

"You're a pig, Tom, just like all men," Pam snapped.

"You know what you need, Pam?" Tom asked while standing up and rolling up his magazine.

"No, Tom, what do I need? Tell me, please."

"You need to get fucked."

Pam's eyes went wide.

Tom saw he'd gotten to her and he kept shooting from the hip. "Yeah, that's right. You need to get fucked long and hard. You need a dick so far up that tight ass of yours that maybe it would loosen you up a little." He turned and pulled his jacket off the back of his chair. "I quit. Get yourself another operator." He waved to George. "See ya, George, don't get eaten out there."

"Yeah, man, same to you," George said with a wave, then he was concentrating on the dials and switches, having to do the work of two men. Tom had already told him he was going to quit, George just hadn't known when. Now Tom had left with a bang. George was planning on leaving, too, but he still hadn't worked up the courage yet. He felt like a coward for deserting the TV station, but with shit going down all over the city, it was time to head for the hills.

"You know, Pam, a bunch of techs have already quit and more are leaving at the end of their shift tonight," George said, while reaching over to play with the switches on Tom's side of the panel.

"Really?" she asked.

George nodded. "I wasn't gonna say anything but I'm gonna get the fuck out of here real soon, too. You should do the same."

"I can't. I'm the station manager. I need to be here until this crisis is over or the place shuts down."

George was getting aggravated now. Pam was being a bitch like always. He turned around to face her, crossed his arms over his chest and said, "Well then, fuck you too. Forget I said anything." then he turned and got back to work, leaving Pam with her mouth hanging open.

Growling under her breath, she turned and walked back out into the studio. Why was everyone acting like even more of an asshole than normal? So what? The dead start to walk and that gives everyone an excuse to be bastards?

The anchorman and scientist were still going at it.

"So let me get this shit straight, Professor, or whatever the fuck you call yourself. What you're saying is that the dead are coming back to life and they want to eat us. That still sounds like horseshit to me. Zombies aren't real, it's make believe."

The scientist frowned deeply. "Please don't use that word. I detest it."

"What? Zombies? That's what you're saying they are."

"Yes, but that word is so childish, it totally lacks the finesse of what the creatures truly are."

"Seriously? I mean, you're not fucking with me here. You're serious. The fucking dead are running around eating people's asses and you want to discuss the semantics over what to call them?"

"Well no, of course not. I'm here to get the word out to the public. People need to know that if one of their loved ones becomes one of these creatures, they need to cut the head off the body immediately or risk being attacked themselves. There's no time to call the police or an ambulance, just cut the head off before the corpse reanimates."

"Whoa, whoa, wait a second here, Doc," the anchorman said, cutting off the scientist from continuing. "Let me get this straight. Here's a scenario for you. Grandpa's sleeping in his room and he has a heart attack in the middle of the night. Grandma wakes up and finds her hubby of fifty years stone cold. What you're saying is she needs to not call the authorities but instead get to a knife and hack off her husband's head before he wakes up and wants to bite her face off?"

"Yes, that's exactly what I'm saying."

The anchorman began to laugh. "Well, man, if that's what you're saying, I have news for you, brainiac. People won't do that. No matter what you tell them, they just won't."

"Then we're all doomed," the scientist said sadly.

A female intern popped up behind the two men and took off her shirt, showing her breasts for the camera as she danced around. The camera operator immediately zoomed in, focusing on the two perfect melons. The right one had a piercing on the nipple, which only added to the sexy sight.

Pam saw the cameraman zooming in and she went to him, tapping him on the shoulder. "Just what do think you're doing?" she demanded.

"Making sure we keep getting high ratings," he added, his eyes never leaving the scope of his camera.

"You need to stop that right now. Put the camera on the professor."

"Fuck that," the cameraman said. "Do you see those tits? Those are perfect. I bet every TV set in the country is on right now and tuned to our channel. Our ratings are gonna go through the roof!"

"But what about the FCC seeing it? They'll fine us millions."

He shrugged, still never making eye contact with Pam, his eyes only for the shapely boobs on his screen. He wasn't alone, every man in the studio—and more than one woman as well—was watching the intern bounce around, all their mouths hanging open.

"Shit, I want a piece of that," another tech said from behind Pam. When she promptly spun around and glared at him, he went back to work, but snuck peeks every few seconds.

"The assholes at the FCC are probably zombie chow by now, so there's no one to fine us," the cameraman said. "That's why Bill's swearing like a trucker." He pulled his eye from the camera and looked Pam right in the eye. "It's the end of the world, baby. Didn't you know that?"

Exasperated, Pam walked away from the man, deciding he had a point. With so much going on in the world, if the FCC wanted to fine them for showing bare boobs on the air, let them.

The scientist and the anchorman were still going at it, and as she watched, it looked like the cool facade of the scientist was slipping. She didn't blame him. Bill was a dick, and wasn't that good of a newsman when you came right down to it, but he was good looking and that's what the station wanted.

"Do you hear yourself?" Bill asked angrily, his face beet-red. "You want people to throw out all sense of right and wrong. What's next? Fucking the recently dead? Why not? If you get them fast enough they're still warm and hey, they don't fight back."

The entire studio stopped and stared at that one, not believing what Bill had just said.

"It sounds to me like someone likes fucking dead women," the scientist said, finally getting in a dig himself. "What the matter? Can't get a live one? Is it because the second they talk to you they find out what an asshole you are?"

"Oh no he didn't," George said from the control booth, doing his best black woman impression again.

"Why you sanctimonious little prick," Bill hissed, and before anyone could do anything, the fuming anchorman lunged at the scientist, attacking him, the two men falling onto the desk, where they rolled around before landing on the floor.

Pam had been holding a clipboard, but she tossed it over her shoulder and threw up her hands. The clipboard landed on its side, bounced a few feet and lay flat, like a dead Frisbee. "It's all falling part. I must be dreaming this shit. Someone needs to pinch me and wake me up."

The cameraman, who was shifting the camera to get a better view, reached out and pinched Pam's left ass cheek.

"What the hell?" she snapped.

"What? I pinched you to show you that you're not dreaming." He was smiling playfully.

Pam slapped his face and walked away. "Asshole, pinch me again and see what'll happen."

As she walked through the studio, she took in the calamity once more. Bill and the scientist were still fighting, while behind them, the intern bounced and danced, gyrating like a belly dancer. All around Pam, people were arguing, yelling and screaming at one another, while others were running back and forth with their heads cut off, doing God knew what.

Upon retuning to the control room, Pam had a look at the screen, where at the bottom, there was a running ticker telling people what rescue stations to go to. There should have been names there such as hospitals, buildings set up as bomb shelters, and schools with gyms, but as Pam read them, she saw locations that were a little different from what she expected.

"George," she said, "would you mind telling me why we're telling people to go to rescue stations such as Gold Rush Strip Club and Sam's Bakery?"

George shrugged. "I figured what the hell. The ones we were broadcasting before weren't relevant, so being so out of date, I figured we should send them somewhere else."

"But a strip club?" Her face grew red with anger. "Why a fucking strip club?"

"Well, I figured if those poor people are gonna die, they might as well get a lap dance before they do."

She rolled her eyes angrily. "Fine, I guess I see a crazy kind of sense to that one. But what about the bakery then? Why send people there?"

George shrugged. "I like pie."

"What? That's it, get out. Get the fuck out of here! You're fired!" she yelled, while grabbing him and pulling him out of his chair. The others in the control room watched silently, not really giving a shit one way or the other.

"Fine," he said angrily. "I was gonna quit anyway. We'll be off the air by tonight, you know. The emergency broadcast networks are gonna take over."

Fuming, she sat down at the control panel and took over George's job. As the man left the control room and walked into the studio, he stopped and talked to three more people. Two of the people left with him, one flipping Pam off as he left. Pam returned the one finger salute and focused on her work.

She looked at the screen to see what was being broadcast over the air. At least Bill and the scientist weren't fighting anymore. Both disheveled, they were sitting back at the desk, talking again. The dancing intern had gotten bored and left, which was a relief to Pam.

Concentrating on the screen, she raised the audio so she could hear better.

"What you people don't seem to understand," the scientist was saying, "is that this is a global event. The dead are walking, for Christ's sake. Do you understand the seriousness of such an occurrence?"

"Of course we do, Doc," Bill said.

"No, I don't think you really do. This is an event that very well may wipe out mankind as we know it. We must all pull together or we're doomed. Doomed!"

"Jesus, Doc, you're being a little over-dramatic, aren't you?" Bill asked.

"No, I most certainly am not. You need to understand something. These dead things kill to eat. Do you get me? They 'eat' their victims and then those victims die and get up and then they go and eat some more, and so on and so on."

"So you're saying these things are cannibals. Hey, guys," he said to the camera and lighting techs. "I wonder if eating a kid is like veal to them, or eating a senior citizen is like eating beef jerky."

"Laugh all you want, but sooner or later these things will overrun us all. There's no way to stop them unless we consider out nuclear arsenal."

"Are you fucking crazy?" Bill asked. Other voices piped in as well.

"No, sir, I'm not crazy. I'm being practical. We need to nuke the cities, destroy the horde where they're gathering in the greatest number. Then, if people dispose of the dead quickly and properly, we may just beat this thing."

Bill threw up his hands, exasperated. "Okay, I've had enough of this nutjob. Pam," he said into the screen. "Can we do something else now?"

Pam pressed a button on the panel and said into a microphone to her left, her voice echoing through speakers mounted on the walls of the studio, "Not yet, Bill, keep talking. That 'nutjob' as you call him, is the best guest speaker we could get on such short notice, and there's no one else to replace him."

"Yeah, because everyone else is probably dead," a tech said from behind Pam.

"Shut up, I wasn't talking to you," she hissed. Then she said into the microphone, "Just keep going till I say to stop."

Bill rolled his eyes and slapped the desk in anger. The scientist didn't seem offended at all from what he'd just heard, and he immediately began giving his speech again, trying to get people to see reason. More people left the studio, walking past the camera and flipping off the viewers at home. Pam wondered who was watching right now. People huddled in their homes, afraid to go outside? One tech passed the camera, turned and pulled his pants, down, mooning the viewers. That got a few laughs from the remaining crew.

"Pam, over here," a voice said from the control room doorway.

Pam looked up and over to see her on-again, off-again boy-friend, Kevin, at the doorway. He was the copilot for the news chopper. He was still learning to fly the chopper though, but he only needed a few more hours under his belt before he could take the final test. At the moment they were in the 'off' part of their relationship.

Pam got up and walked over to him, after gesturing for an-other tech in the small room to take over the control panel. "What do want, Kevin?" she asked when she was less than a foot from him.

"What I want is to be rich and famous, but I'll settle for living to see the sun come up tomorrow."

Pam sighed. Kevin said shit like that all the time.

"Okay, sorry, I'm nervous is all. I just came back from doing a run. Pam, it's wild out there. People everywhere, fires burning out of control, people eating people. Shit, it's like a fucking zombie movie out there."

Pam rolled her eyes, something she was fond of doing. To her, everyone else was an idiot, and only she was the smart one. "Zombie movies are for idiots, Kevin, you know that. The idea that zombies are real is for geeks with acne all over their face that live in their mother's basements and play video games all day because they don't have a girlfriend or God-forbid, a wife." She turned and looked out across the control room, as if there was an imaginary camera there, as if she was being watched by unknown people, perhaps people even reading this story. "Yeah, that's what I said, assholes, I'm talking to you, you nerds. Get a life, get a woman and go live life and stop reading about zombies. Grow the fuck up!"

Kevin watched her and blinked, not understanding what she was doing. When she turned back to face him, she said, "Sorry, just something I do sometimes when I get aggravated, you know that."

"Yeah, and it freaks me out every time," Kevin said. "So listen, ten o'clock tonight be on the roof. We're gonna steal the news chopper and get the hell out of the city. Boston is fucked; it's time to go to the White Mountains or somewhere empty of people."

"You want to do what? Kevin, you can't do that, 'we' can't do that. It's stealing," she said.

"Who gives a shit? Listen, Pam, by tomorrow this city is gonna be nothing but those things out there. They're everywhere and…" He looked down, as if he wanted to say something else.

"And what? Say it, Kevin, what?" She gave him a suspicious look. "And why did you pick me to go with you? We're not exactly an item anymore."

"Well, and I want you there with me 'cause if you're not, then I'm gonna have to jerk off all the time. I want you there so I have a chick to bang. You should consider yourself lucky; I could take any woman with me."

"So let me get this straight," she said, crossing her arms angrily. "It's either stay in the city and probably die by flesh-eating cannibals, or I can go with you and escape but I'll have to fuck you to pay my way? Basically whore myself out to you?"

Kevin looked a little sorry. "Well, if you put it that way I guess it does sound kind of shitty. But look at it this way. Whenever I took you out for dinner and a movie you would always at least give me a blowjob or worse, a hand job, if we didn't go back to my place and fuck. Basically you had sex with me for dinner and a movie. Isn't that the same thing? You got to see a film and were fed, and in return I got some head."

Pam glared at him, having to admit deep down he had a point there. In many ways, women were simple whores, who got paid in different ways for putting out—just not outright with cash, but food, movies and presents were all fair game.

Yes, that's right, she could spin it all she wanted, but it was what it was. She wanted to punch him, but others in the control room were looking and she could tell a few were listening to their conversation.

"Fine, I'll go with you," she said in a hushed tone so as not to be overheard. "But I'm telling you now, nothing in the butt. Promise me."

Kevin made a face, wincing. Shit, he figured with them in the hills, only the two of them, he would finally get some more butt sex. He and her had done it once, and she hadn't been at all happy about it. He had enjoyed it immensely however.

"Okay, I'll agree to that, but I have to be honest, I asked one more person to come with us."

"Who?"

"Dodger is coming, too."

"That asshole?" she asked.

"Hey, he may be an asshole but he works for SWAT, and having a guy like him around will come in handy. I don't know how to use a gun and you don't either."

She thought it over for a moment and finally nodded. "Okay, he can come, but I'm telling you right now, no threesomes; it's not gonna happen. Agreed?"

"Why don't we discuss that one some more later. After all, it's gonna get lonely in the hills. You might change your mind."

She squeezed her arms tighter over her chest. "No, I won't. I'd never fuck that asshole."

Chapter 2

The apartment building on the edge of Dorchester had been built in the 1960's. At the time of its completion, the building had been considered a high-end, luxury destination for the well-off of Boston. For ten years it was just that, but then the developer hit a rough patch from gambling and he had to sell off a lot of his holdings or risk going swimming with a pair of cement shoes.

Not wanting to go out like that, the developer quickly sold the apartment building to the first one with cash in hand.

That person had been a clown named Bobo.

Bobo had left the circus after years of making millions smile. Though he was retired, he still liked to do benefits if asked—and offered enough money. Bobo had done such a benefit one time and had been seriously hurt. A lawyer had gotten the clown a hefty sum and Bobo had decided to buy the apartment building with most of his financial windfall.

Then he had kicked out the people that lived there and invited all his clown friends to come live with him. That was how the clown commune was born, with over three hundred clowns under one roof.

Bright white spotlights lit up the side of the building, but these lights weren't from a big top. They belonged to Boston's finest, who after getting word that the clowns were keeping their dead in the basement, and after asking the clowns to evacuate only to have them refuse, the police had no choice but to go in and rectify the situation immediately.

"Bobo, this is the police," Captain Alexander said through a bullhorn. "I know you've been keeping an eye on what's been going on and you know why we're here. This is your last warning. Evacuate the building or my men and I are coming in."

A skinny man with blonde hair wearing a SWAT uniform came up behind the captain and patted him on the shoulder to get the man's attention. "Why are we fucking around here anyway, Captain? Is it because they're keeping the dead in the basement that have become zombies?"

"Nah, Dodger," the captain said, lowering the bullhorn so he could talk without it being broadcast across the area. "I just hate fucking clowns."

The captain turned back to the building and raised the bullhorn to his mouth again. "Bobo, this is your last warning. You have five minutes and then the shit's gonna hit the fan."

Suddenly, every light in the building's windows went out as the tenants got ready for the invasion. The captain looked over his shoulder at Dodger and said, "Get your men ready, Sergeant; you're goin' inside in four minutes."

"Got it, Captain. I can't believe they're gonna resist us on this, we're doing this for their own good."

The captain had turned away and was saying into the bullhorn. "Bobo, it doesn't have to be this way. No one has to get hurt. You have less than five minutes now, Bobo, don't be a fool, cooperate with us."

"Goddamn stupid clowns," Dodger said under his breath as he turned to get ready for the breach of the building.

"Oh, and Sergeant Dodger," the captain called.

"Yeah?"

"Be careful in there. Remember, these are clowns you're dealing with. They're not like normal people. Who knows what kind of sick shit they're into."

"Don't I know it, Captain." Dodger left then, crossing the parking lot to where a dozen men were waiting for their orders. All the men wore SWAT uniforms, bullet proof vests, and were armed to the teeth. When they saw Dodger coming their way, they all stopped what they were doing and waited.

"So, Sarge, we going in or what?" a bearded man asked Dodger. Though it was night, he wore dark sunglasses.

"Yeah, we're going in now," Dodger said. "So gather your shit and follow me." The men took less than thirty seconds to grab their gear, then in a loose line, Dodger led them to the rear of the building. "Regular police are gonna hit the front while we go in through the back and onto the roof by grappling lines," Dodger explained. His face grew hard. "Remember, guys, these are clowns we're dealing with. These aren't normal people. So watch your back and watch your buddy's back."

"We're not afraid of a bunch of fucking clowns, Sergeant," one of the men said and the others agreed, grunting and hooting to get psyched up for the invasion.

Suddenly, the radio on Dodger's vest began to crackle, followed by the captain's voice yelling, "Everyone move in now! All units into the building!"

"Okay, let's go," Dodger said and began running while staying low, his rifle held before him. His men followed, and when Dodger pointed to the right, to the side of the building, six of the men veered off and with grappling hooks, sent the lines high and began climbing.

One of the men was almost to the edge of the roof when a clown appeared. Pasty-faced, with big red lips, pink hair, and a yellow jumpsuit, he was the epitome of what a clown should look like.

"Here, let me give you a hand," the clown said to the SWAT trooper, who assumed that this particular clown was on the side of the police and wanted to help. The trooper reached up for the proffered hand, and as he eased off some of his weight from the hand holding the line, something happened he didn't understand.

There was a soft 'pop' and the hand came free from the clown's arm, and suddenly the trooper found himself falling backwards, the plastic hand still in his grip, as if by holding the toy hand, it might somehow save him. As the man fell to his death, the clown laughed loud, his real hand popping back out of the loose shirt-sleeve. Then he turned and skipped away, singing a happy tune.

Dodger was just about to enter the building when the trooper landed a few feet from him. With a meaty splat the body exploded, spraying blood and guts in all directions. Some hit Dodger and he made a disgusted face. "Ah, gross," he said. "That's so nasty." He was the last one in the building, his men taking the stairs two at a time. As Dodger entered the stairwell and began climbing, a shadow crossed the landing above him. Coming around the stairwell with his rifle up, he saw another clown, this one wearing a purple jumpsuit with 'balloon' pants and bright red hair, a red nose and dark blue lips, white pancake makeup covering the face completing the look. The clown held a giant red hammer in his hands, and as Dodger raised the rifle, the hammer came down on Dodger's head. But instead of feeling the crushing pain of a flattened skull, the hammer squeaked, and Dodger felt something soft hit him. It was an inflatable hammer.

"Take that, you awful, awful man," the clown said in a high-pitched voice. "Leave us alone, we have a right to be here." The clown pulled a handgun from behind his back and Dodger shot him in the chest. The handgun fired once, the muzzle aimed right at Dodger's face, but no bullet hit him in the forehead. Instead, a cloth flag popped out with the word **BANG!** written on it in colorful letters. The clown sank to the floor, dead, shitting his pants in loud, wet sounds that filled the stairwell. Dodger gasped at the smell and tried to breathe through his nose. The clown wouldn't stop shitting and farting, the crotch of his jumpsuit rippling with each blast.

"Fucking clowns, they're all crazy," Dodger said. He began descending the stairs to join his men.

In the hallways of the apartment complex, chaos reigned. Clowns were everywhere, and of all shapes and sizes. Some wore makeup while others went with masks. Some had long red shoes three times the size of their normal feet, and others wore sneakers. Animal balloons were everywhere, the SWAT team kicking them in the air or just stepping on them

Three troopers had broken off from their team to search along the hallway, when suddenly a door opened and there before the men stood a mime. Before the mime could do anything, the lead trooper shot the mime in the face, sending him flying backwards to land in a heap on the floor with half his head missing, his brains painting the floor dark red.

The second trooper in line moved up to the first and said, "I saw that mime open the door. Was he a zombie? Is that why you killed him?"

The first trooper snorted as he gazed back at his buddy. "He wasn't a zombie. He was a *mime*, and in my book that's a hell of a lot worse than being dead and wanting to eat people." The trooper began walking down the hallway, leaving the second trooper watching his back and not quite understanding. Then his face lit up and he nodded, agreeing completely. "Yeah, you're right; mimes do suck ass."

"Told ya," the first trooper said as he kicked in another door. Three midget clowns and a poodle all turned as one and began talking and barking at once, all outraged that their door had been kicked in.

"Yeah, yeah, save it for the big top, guys, I'm not interested." He gestured with the muzzle of his rifle for them to leave the apartment and go into the hall. "Move it."

Not having a choice, the height-deprived clowns exited the room and were soon being ushered down the hallway, one of the clowns holding the poodle in its arms. The first trooper was about to leave when he heard a loud thump coming from a back room. Footsteps sounded behind him and he turned to see another trooper there. "Shit, Dodger, you almost made me shoot you," he said.

"Sorry, Don, I thought you heard me," Dodger said. "What you got here?"

"Three midgets and a poodle, all gone, but I heard something coming from down that way," Don said, gesturing with the muzzle of his rifle.

" 'Three midgets and a poodle.' It sounds like the beginnings of a bad joke," Dodger said as he moved closer to Don. He gestured with his chin for Don to lead the way, as Don was the one who'd heard the sound. Don nodded and crossed the room and entered a small hallway, Dodger right behind him.

"I ever tell you I wanted to be a clown when I was a kid, Dodger?" Don asked.

"Don't tell the captain, that, Don, he fucking hates clowns."

"You know, I hear that shit all the time and I don't get it. Clowns are happy and funny and love to make people smile."

Dodger frowned. "Don, clowns are creepy and scary and frankly, I bet a lot of them are closet pedophiles. I mean think about it. What better way to get close to kids than to be a clown? Birthdays, circuses, shit, wherever clowns are kids are sure to be there."

Don stopped walking and turned so he could look Dodger in the eyes. "All clowns aren't pedophiles; that's ridiculous."

"I didn't say 'all' clowns, just some of them," Dodger rebutted.

Another thump caused both men to ignore their discussion and focus on the door before them.

"What do you think?" Dodger asked, his eyes darting from Don to the closed door.

"Only one way to find out," Don replied, and in one smooth motion, he raised his right foot high and kicked in the door, the bottom of his combat boot connecting with the door right below the doorknob. In a loud crash and splintering wood, the door was thrown inward, Don coming down on both feet and charging inside, Dodger right behind him.

Don went to the right and Dodger to the left, both men leveling rifles at whatever was waiting within the room. Neither man was ready for what was there, however, and both stopped in shock and horror, their mouths falling open at the sight before them.

Sitting on the floor of the small eat-in kitchen, was the fattest clown either man had ever seen. The clown was male and must have weighed over four hundred pounds. The clown's attire consisted of what was basically a giant-sized muumuu, the colors a mix of yellow, blue and red. But the red wasn't from the material, but was from the blood of a smaller clown the fat one held in his arms, as he chewed on the small body as if it was a night-time snack before bed. The smaller clown had no head, and where it had disappeared to was anyone's guess. The fat one was chewing at the insides of the smaller one, tearing at the organs and swallowing them without chewing. Blood coated the entire face of the fat one, the crimson liquid meshing with the white-painted face to make it a watered-down version of what the clown was supposed to look like.

As the two troopers burst into the room, the fat clown looked up and seemed to smile, just as he slurped up the long intestine he'd been gobbling down. Neither trooper could tell if the clown was alive or dead, thanks to the pancake makeup, but from what they had seen in the past since the dead began to walk, it was a pretty good bet the fat guy was already dead and had revived.

Dodger put his arm over his nose and mouth to try and stop the smell of feces and blood permeating his senses, but even with his arm pressed to his nose it barely did anything. Even before death the clown had been a stinky son of a bitch, far too fat to even fit into the shower, let alone be able to reach around and wipe his ass.

Don was thinking in a similar vein. "Jesus Christ, will you look at the size of this fucker?" he said. "How in God's name did this guy manage to wipe his ass?"

"He probably didn't," Dodger said, his voice muffled behind his arm.

The fat clown had pushed the smaller clown corpse off him and was trying to crawl towards the two troopers. The bulk heaved and swayed, undulating like a giant blob of flesh.

The two men took a step back, their eyes locked on the behemoth before them.

"Well, don't just stand there," Dodger told Don, "Shoot the guy in the head man, the head!"

"I know, I know, I've seen enough movies to know that."

"Movies? What does this have to do with movies?" Dodger asked, confused.

Don ignored the question. "Never mind, it doesn't matter." He moved the rifle muzzle a little to the left to line it up with the head of the clown. Next to the giant bulk, the head was small and seemed not to fit at all with the torso, as if it had been attached there by accident.

The clown slid forwards another foot, and Don took a step back out of instinct. It was as he was about to shoot that he felt pressure on his left boot, right where his ankle was located. He looked down to see that he'd found the severed head of the smaller clown, and that the head was still very active. The teeth on the head had clamped down on Don's boot, the jaws locking so that the head was firmly attached. Don screamed and began running around the kitchen, the head bouncing and flapping as it held on tight. To Dodger, who suddenly saw Don screaming and running around the room for no apparent reason, he looked on with curiosity. Then he spotted the head attached to Don's boot, but to him, as Don was moving so fast, it looked like there was a small white ball there, thanks to the clown's painted face.

"Get it off me! Get it off me!" Don screamed as he ran around the room, trying to separate the head from his boot, with no luck whatsoever. He ran in a skip, the head flapping back and forth as the clown's teeth held on for the long haul.

"Damn it, Don, hold still!" Dodger yelled, wanting to smack the head with the butt of his rifle, only Don wouldn't stop moving. The panicked trooper then went too close to the fat clown and suddenly he was falling, thanks to the weight-challenged clown grabbing Don's other leg. Don fell heavily onto the floor and rolled immediately to his side. The severed head was still there and the fat clown was pulling Don close, ready to begin eating again.

Don stared helplessly, in shock, as his right leg was drawn closer and closer to the red mouth of fatso. Then, just when he thought it was too late and the clown was about to chomp down on his leg as if it was a chicken leg, a loud report filled the room and the clown's face imploded, to then blow out the back of the skull in a bloody mess of blood and brain matter. Bits of flecked bone was mixed in with the goop, and it all slid down the cabinets behind the now very dead clown.

Don used his free leg—after pulling it out of the clown's grasp—to kick the severed head off his left boot with the heel of his right one. It bounced across the floor to rebound off the wall, where it spun in a circle three times. Dodger went over to the head, picked it up, then began darting to the left and right, the head in his hands like a basketball. He raised it in a jump shot and let it fly. The head soared across the kitchen, bounced off the far wall, then landed in the small trash can located there.

"Booyah, a three-pointer if there ever was one," Dodger said, pumping a fist in the air. He went to Don and helped the shaken trooper up. "Better be more careful there, pal," he told Don as the man straightened his uniform and picked up his rifle from where it had fallen in his panic.

Screams filtered in from the hallway and Dodger patted Don on the shoulder. "Come on, man, looks like there's more shit to do before we can wrap this operation up for the night."

"I'm with you. I just got a hell of a scare there. Thanks for having my back," Don said as the two troopers began exiting the apartment.

"It's cool, man," Dodger replied, and in seconds the two men were outside, and back in the main hallway, where chaos reigned. Someone had let loose with gas canisters, and tear gas filled the air, flowing up and down the hallways on each floor.

"Masks, man, get on your mask!" Dodger yelled as he did just that, Don doing the same.

A clown with pink hair stumbled out of an apartment at the far end of the hallway and it was clear to all he was a zombie. The troopers opened up, blowing the clown's chest to pieces, the clown falling back against the wall to then slide down it.

The gas swirled and the clown was lost from sight, and at the same time another door opened perpendicular to the fallen clown and out came a woman, who from the way she looked and acted, had to be the dead clown's wife. She was also in clown makeup, and wore a bright red suit with long feet and a flower on her lapel. She ran to the fallen clown, calling his name, while the same clown began to rise again.

"Oh, Roberto, thank God you're okay," the clown woman said.

"Get back, lady, that guy's dead!" Dodger yelled as the woman embraced her fallen husband in a fierce hug.

The clown's head lowered so that his teeth were even with his wife's arm, and before anyone could stop him, the clown took a bite out of the arm, tearing into it and pulling back the skin, which pulled and flexed like rubber while the material of the suit was torn. Strangely, there was no blood.

"Oh sweet Jesus," Dodger said and ran at the two clowns, grabbing the man and shoving him away from his wife, who for some reason wasn't screaming, despite the chunk of flesh missing from her arm.

As the clown was pushed to the side, Dodger pointed and yelled, "Kill that son of a bitch for good this time!"

Three troopers along with Don opened up, riddling the clown with bullets. The body danced a jig of death before a few rounds found his head, then the clown dropped to the floor, dead for good.

"Are you all right?" Dodger asked as he grabbed the woman and looked at her arm through his gas mask.

She looked perplexed for a second, not understanding why Dodger was so concerned, then she realized what he referred to and she nodded knowingly. "I'm fine, hon, see?" She popped the arm from her side. It was fake. "But I have to admit, I'm pretty damn mad that you killed my husband. We were a duo, you know. Now who am I going to do the Goldberg's bar mitzvah with next week?" She pulled out a horn, honked it twice, and ran off into the swirling tear gas.

Dodger watched her go, shaking his head. "They're all fucking crazy," he said. "Completely bonkers."

Don moved up beside him, his voice garbled from the gas mask. "They're clowns, what did you expect?"

Six troopers were at the far end of the hallway, and together they forced down a door to another apartment. Inside, they found six clowns, three adults and three children, all wearing the garb of their calling. One was no older than five, with bright blue hair and a red nose, carrying a balloon animal as the family couldn't afford a stuffed one. It was horrible to see. What was it like to be a child trapped in a commune full of clowns? He had a feeling it wasn't as jolly as one might think, and was probably torture for many. The clowns were herded out of the room one at a time. When one passed Dodger, he smiled widely and then squeezed a flower on his chest. Water shot from the flower, hitting the clear plastic of the mask over Dodger's eyes. Before Dodger could react, the clown was past him, being shoved with the rest of the clowns by the other troopers.

The hallway seemed to become calmer for a few seconds, and Dodger wondered if maybe it was all almost over, when a tall clown in a bright yellow suit and no hair, the pate as bald as could be, ran out of an apartment door, laughing loudly, while behind him another clown, a female this time, ran after him, yelling for him to stop. She held a wig of bright blue hair in her left hand. She wanted her man to put his hair on before going out. It was a clown's credo: always stay in character.

As the man ran at Dodger, the trooper raised the butt of his rifle and whacked the clown in the nose. The clown went down hard, blood gushing from his broken nose.

"Laugh that off, Bozo," Dodger said as the wife ran up to her fallen husband. Three troopers helped the clown up and escorted the couple away.

"Jesus, I need a break," Dodger said as he walked down the hallway to the fire stairs, then began descending them. He needed a place that was devoid of people. Somewhere where he could gather himself. The gas mask was too tight on his face and he was getting a headache. He eventually found himself in the basement; he went to an old water basin and leaned over it, retching as he took his mask off, the taste of bile bitter in his mouth.

"Jesus Christ," he muttered. "Fucking clowns."

"Hey, man, you're not alone down here, ya know," a voice said, high-pitched and nasally.

Dodger glanced up to see a fat black trooper with short dark hair and the beginnings of a beard. He had two chins as well, but the eyes were friendly enough.

"Sorry, I just needed someplace to take a rest, ya know?" Dodger said.

"Yeah, man, I know what you mean. This is my second week on the job. Would you believe it? Two weeks the fucking dead start running around and now this. Clowns, man, ain't that some shit."

"Yeah, I know what you mean," Dodger said.

"I'm Pete by the way," the fat trooper said as he walked over and held out a hand for Dodger, who took the proffered hand and shook it. Dodger tried not to wince at the sweaty palm.

Dodger had a better look at Pete. As he eyed the obese black cop, he had to wonder how the guy had ever gotten into the academy let alone passed. He had to ask, "How the hell did you get on the force looking like *that* anyway?"

Pete shrugged. "My uncle is the captain over at the 57th Precinct. He pulled a few strings to get me into the academy, then a few more to make the brass look the other way in the physical part of training."

"Nice," Dodger said. "I get into a bind and I'll have your fat ass to cover me. What the hell are you supposed to do if you need to chase someone? Something tells me you're not too light on your feet."

Pete pulled his handgun. "That's what God made these for, man. I wouldn't run like an idiot, I'd just shoot the fucker in the back."

"Nice," Dodger repeated, saying it sarcastically.

Pete pulled out a joint and lit up, taking a deep drag and exhaling. "Ah, that's smooth, man." He noticed Dodger staring at him so he held the joint out, offering it to Dodger. "Oh shit, sorry, man. You want some?"

Dodger was about to snap at the fat man, and tell him to put out the damn joint, when he suddenly realized how silly that would sound. The dead were walking. He was in a building full of zombie clowns. Shit, getting high seemed like a pretty damn good idea at the moment. "Yeah, give it here," he finally said.

Pete handed it over and Dodger took a hit, then closed his eyes and let the feeling wash over him. He handed it back and Pete took another hit as well. For a few minutes, neither man spoke, just passed the joint back and forth.

"You gonna run, Pete?" Dodger finally asked the fat, black man standing next to him, breaking the silence between them. He lit a cigarette and snapped his Zippo closed. He took a pull and let it out, the smoke drifting lazily into the dingy basement air. In the background, gunshots could be heard and screams for help as the rest of the SWAT team cleared out the apartment building of any remaining clowns. He shivered at the thought. Zombie clowns; what a terrible combination.

Why the hell had the clown commune kept their dead with them? It made no sense, and now there was chaos in the rundown building.

The fat man with the dark face shrugged slightly, not replying to Dodger's question. Truth was, Pete didn't know where the other man was going with his question. To run would be to abandon his post; to take the coward's way out, and for all he knew, Dodger was trying to set him up. He didn't know Dodger, the two troopers assigned to different units, and he'd just met the man, and though he'd sized Dodger up as an okay guy, Pete could be wrong. But they'd just smoked a joint together so Pete figured Dodger couldn't be all bad.

As if Dodger sensed Pete's internal thoughts, he said, "I don't mean anything by it, was just wondering is all." Dodger shrugged then as he looked over at Pete. This large fat man was a sight to see. His clothes didn't fit, his sleeves far too short, and rolls of fat could be seen under his bullet proof vest. He was easily twice as wide as Dodger and he exuded a strong odor of pastrami or garlic or something from a deli. But despite all this, Dodger liked the man immediately. He figured he could fight by Pete's side, and Dodger figured that if he did run tonight, this man would be good to have with him to watch his back, that is, if Pete didn't try to eat Dodger first.

"I hadn't really given it much thought, but If I did…" Pete trailed off.

"I could run tonight if I really wanted to," Dodger explained. "A friend of mine works for a local Boston news station. He flies the news chopper, and said I could come along when he leaves the city tonight with his girlfriend."

Pete said nothing, only stared with small eyes at Dodger.

Swallowing, Dodger said, "You think it's right to take off? To get the hell out of the city?"

Pete said nothing. Instead, he swung his rifle up, his attention focused on the door leading out of the basement. Dodger dropped his cigarette to the floor, stepped on it out of habit, and turned to see what the fat man was so interested in.

Then he heard the sound.

From across the room where the door was located, came a shuffling sound, along with the added noise of squeaking and wheezing. It was a chilling sound and both troopers readied their rifles, prepared for what they assumed was coming.

What took seconds felt like an hour, but finally the door slowly began to open, the creaking hinges filling the air with a high-pitched wailing. A hand appeared, pale and withered from age, then the rest of the body, the small form garbed in the familiar attire of a clown. The sound of labored breathing was added to the other sounds.

Dodger's trigger finger was ready to close, the emerging figure about to be sprayed with bullets, when something made Dodger stop. He darted out a hand and pushed Pete's rifle down. "No, don't shoot," he said softly.

"Why not?" Pete asked. His head was spinning. "Man, that was good hash.

"Because that fucker ain't dead, that's why?"

The figure emerged from within the doorway and Dodger nodded when he knew he was right. The clown wasn't one of the dead, though he was missing his left leg, and the material of the clown suit on that leg swung back and forth.

"Of course I'm not dead, damn it," the clown said, his voice hoarse and cracking.

Dodger could tell the clown was old, well into his seventies if not older.

Hobbling with a crutch, the old clown hopped up to the two troopers. "You two with the others?" he asked, eyeing the two men.

Dodger nodded.

"Well, good luck with that." The old clown began hobbling away, then he stopped and turned to face the two men again. "Say, did you hear about the one-legged man who got a job in a brewery?"

"No," Pete replied.

"He's making hops," the clown said, a wide smile creasing his pale face. "Tell me this… What do you tell a one-legged hitch-hiker?"

"I don't know, what?" Dodger asked, his face serious.

"You tell him to 'hop' in," the clown said, laughing loud and long.

Both Dodger and Pete made a face, wincing together.

"Oh man, that's bad," Dodger said.

"Where do one-legged people eat?" the clown asked, barely able to get out the words, he was laughing so hard.

"I don't want to know," Pete said.

"I-HOP. Where else?" the clown cackled.

Dodger raised his rifle. "I swear, old man, one more joke and I'm gonna shoot you."

The old clown acted like he didn't hear Dodger's warning and said, "Why did the bunny hop around on one leg?"

"No, please, no more lame jokes," Pete said, moaning as he rolled his eyes.

"Because the other one was on a key chain!" the clown roared, bending over and almost falling, he was laughing so hard.

The two troopers stood still, not so much as a hint of a smile on their faces.

Finally the clown slowed his laughter and wiped a tear from an eye. "You boys need to lighten up a bit. I only got one leg, and I figure if I can't laugh at myself, who can? Hell, I can't even outrun the dead like this. I'll be the first to get caught once I'm made to leave this building."

"No, that's not true," Pete said. "We'll take you somewhere safe."

"Sure you will, sonny," the clown replied. "But don't mind me if I'm a little distrustful of the authorities." He turned and began walking away, then paused at the doorway at the opposite side of the room from the one he'd entered in. "You know that the clowns here are keeping the dead in the basement, right? There's a whole room full of 'em; everyone that's died in the past week or so is there. Fucked up I know, but what're you gonna do. Listen, Bobo's dead, so you won't have much trouble getting everyone to do what you want now."

"Thanks, we'll check it out," Dodger said.

"Yeah, you do that," the old clown said just before he slipped into the doorway, the hobbling, shuffling sound of the crutch and one leg echoing off the cracked stone walls. "You do that," he repeated, his voice fading to nothing.

Chapter 3

When Pete and Dodger finally reached the basement entrance, more troopers were already there, working to tear off the boards that had been nailed over the door. The wood was an assortment of scrap, everything from an old table to pieces of a door frame, to two-by-fours of odd sizes. It had all been nailed quickly, with much haste, and so it didn't take too long for the troopers to take it all down, thanks to some pry bars and their hands.

Behind the working men, the rest of the squad waited silently. They were freaked out to the say the least. Clowns were bad enough but zombie clowns was too much for some of them. They knew their dreams would be filled with the pale dead faces of clowns for many nights to come.

Soon, almost all the support boards that were holding up the majority of the barricade were removed, until one at a time the rest were taken off until only one strong board remained to hold back the rest of the makeshift barricade. Dodger swallowed the knot in his throat as he watched the last board pulled free, the rending of the nails sliding out of the doorframe reminiscent of fingernails on a chalkboard.

And then it was like a tidal wave of human flesh was coming through the remaining barricade, the wood falling apart now that it wasn't attached to the doorframe. White hands shot through any hole in the barricade, and pasty-white faces with red and blue noses could be seen as well. Moaning mixed with a chilling laughter floated in the air.

Undead clown after undead clown filled the hallway, each reaching for the troopers, who began fighting back, many in the front quickly taken down by the comical onslaught.

"Retreat, retreat!" someone yelled and quickly the troopers began to fall back, some going up the stairs and others further down the hallway. Soon the troopers had room to move, if only just, and they began to shoot at the slowly, shambling clowns. Red noses were pulped as bullets hit home and colorful wigs were blasted off heads with brains still inside them. But still the undead clowns surged forward, hands opening and closing to grasp their prey.

Pete and Dodger were in the midst of it all, punching and shooting as best they could. Dodger could see it was a losing battle and he managed to grab Pete and pull the fat black man along with him. Clowns lunged at them from all sides and Dodger used the butt of his rifle to knock them away. Pete wasn't as brave but the man did his best to fight off the moaning, laughing clowns.

The undead clowns began to spread out from their initial clump, and once this happened, the troopers gained the upper hand, quickly shooting them down in twos and threes. When the last colorful zombie was down, Dodger and Pete, along with a few more souls made of sterner stuff, entered the basement to see what was waiting within.

Amidst boxes marked 'Xmas' and other debris usually found in a basement, such as an old baby carriage and a stained and torn mattress, were the remnants of a hundred bodies, all torn apart and gutted. But despite this the corpses still moved and twitched, while undead clowns moved amongst them, picking up a juicy leg here or a fat arm there. Sharp teeth sank into the tender flesh of the bodies, as the undead clowns fed on the meat around them.

Dodger took over with the distasteful chore of shooting the clowns in the head, and when one zombie close with pink hair and a blue nose began to crawl towards him, he calmly began to reload. Bile filled his mouth as he slid fresh bullets into the cylinder. Even with their pasty makeup, most of the clowns still looked human, and it sickened him to have to put them down. But they weren't human anymore, and though he told himself that again and again, it was still hard to face.

As the pink-haired clown reached out for Dodger's boot, Pete stepped up to join Dodger and aimed his revolver at its head. The gunshot filled the air, all the more deafening because of the close confines of the stone walls. The head exploded from the point blank impact of the bullet and the clown dropped to the floor in a spray of blood, brains and strands of pink wig.

Dodger snapped the cylinder closed on his gun and began firing again. When he was finished, he turned to Pete, his eyes vacant. In all his years on the force, he never would have imagined that he'd be in a situation such as this. It was an emotional moment for him, and Dodger was glad he had at least Pete there to share it with him, to be another soul who understood what he was feeling.

Pete's face was scrunched up as he said, "I need to use the bathroom. I can't wait anymore. I swear, I'm crowning now." Before Dodger could reply, Pete was running off, searching for a bathroom.

"You've got to be kidding me," Dodger said in amazement, as the fat trooper waddled off, his butt cheeks squeezed tightly together.

Pete found an empty apartment on the first floor and he ran inside and right to the bathroom. If there had been a zombie somewhere in the place it would have gotten him for sure. Once inside the bathroom, it took a few minutes for him to get his uniform off, the SWAT gear bulky and connected with straps. He swore he was going to crap his pants, and when he finally dropped trou, he was already shitting as his butt hit the toilet seat.

His face instantly took on a look of peace as he voided his bowls. His nose scrunched up and he thought back to that rice bowl he'd gotten at KFC the previous night. "Man, it smelled better going in," he commented as he filled the bowl to the point he had to flush once just to make sure it didn't clog.

When the initial blast was over, he got a better look at the bathroom. It was done in white tile but other than that it looked like a circus tent had been thrown up. Red and blue curtains over the window, a yellow shower curtain and bath rug, and pictures of clowns on all three walls—the last wall being for the shower and tub insert.

"Jesus, clowns are bad decorators," he mumbled as he began rolling toilet paper around his hand to start the arduous task of wiping himself. Water had splashed up from the bowl and now coated his ass, and as he began wiping, he miscalculated and got some on his fingers. "Seriously?" he mumbled as he inspected his hand. He sniffed it experimentally. What was it about a person that they liked the smell of their own shit? he wondered. He knew he loved the odor of his farts and when he would be on the couch watching TV and he farted, he would always close the blanket tight and stick his nose under the covers to get a good whiff. Sometimes he would just stick his hand over his asshole when he was going to fart, then it would coat his hand good. He would quickly pull it up and then take a good inhale, enjoying the smell. (Oh please, don't be so smug; you know you do it, too.)

The sink was next to the toilet, and he managed to get the water on and wash his hand, then he wiped it on a purple tower hanging beside the sink and finished wiping his butt. When he was satisfied he was as clean as he could get, and had used up half a roll of toilet paper, he got dressed and left the bathroom, the miasma of the KFC rice bowl floating in the air like a toxic cloud.

He was fidgeting with his belt and uniform as he entered the hallway, so he didn't notice there was someone standing at the end, wreathed in shadows, until he looked up. "Hey you," he said, doing his best to hide the fact he'd been startled. "You can't be in here. Everyone needs to evacuate this place."

The figure didn't move, not so much as a twitch, and Pete moved forward a few steps. His rifle was slung over his shoulder, and in the confines of the hallway, it wouldn't be easy to unsling, especially due to his wide girth.

"Did you hear what I said? You gotta leave, man."

Still the figure remained motionless. Pete reached down and pulled a small flashlight from his utility belt and flicked on the beam. The thin white light pierced the gloom of the hallway and illuminated the figure before him. The beam hit around the knees first and Pete sighed, seeing it was yet another clown. The pants on this clown were yellow with bits of red coating it, like something liquid and crimson in color had dripped down from above. Pete paid this no mind, having seen far too many elaborate clown costumes in one night already. He began raising the beam, slowly moving up the legs and the torso of the immobile clown.

"Come on, buddy, you gotta leave," Pete said just as the light hit the clown's face and Pete stopped moving, his jaw falling open as he took in the countenance of the figure before him.

The term 'evil clown' came to mind as Pete stared at the frightening visage before him; he felt his knees go weak.

The clown wasn't dead, or at least Pete didn't think so. The terrible face was something out of a nightmare, the features that should have been meant for children's birthday parties or fun at the circus, distorted into something malevolent.

The mouth had been sliced on both sides nearly up to the eyes, and as the clown smiled, both sides of its face split in half, showing the muscle and tendons beneath the torn flesh. Slowly the evil clown raised a bloody knife he held in his right hand and as the tongue slid out of the gaping mouth; he licked the knife clean, slurping the fluid like a child sucking on a lollipop.

"Drop the knife, now," Pete said, his voice shaking.

Was it Pete's imagination or did the clown's eyes glow red in the beam of the flashlight?

The clown stopped sucking the knife and began to laugh, long and loud. Maniacal would be the best way to describe the laughter, but there was nothing jovial about it.

Then the clown was moving forward, picking up speed with each step. Bells on the clown's shoes jangled with each footstep, the sound chilling when added to the macabre sight before Pete.

"Stop, don't move!" Pete yelled as he tried to swing his rifle around. He wore a revolver as a sidearm but he was too frazzled to remember to grab it.

Laughing even louder, shrilly and high-pitched, the clown charged forward, the knife held out before it, the mouth pulled wide in a rictus of a smile, the tendons reflecting what light there was left after Pete dropped the flashlight to maneuver his rifle. But as the clown came at him, Pete knew he wasn't going to be fast enough. Hell, he was so damn fat the term 'fast' wasn't even in his vocabulary.

The clown was only a few feet away, the knife held high to gut Pete, when suddenly, a pale hand shot out of another open doorway and grabbed the clown's foot at the ankle. The grip was tight and the evil clown went falling face first to the floor. Wanting to halt his fall, the clown threw his hands out before him, but the knife was in one of them still and the blade got twisted around. It was now pointing upwards! The clown fell onto the blade, the tip slicing into his heart and killing him instantly. As blood seeped out from beneath the body, and the legs twitched a few times in spasms, Pete stood stock still, staring, his mouth hanging wide open like a landed fish.

He didn't move until the clown began to stir again, reanimating, becoming one of the undead, the head slowly rising off the floor. Another trooper appeared and spotted the clown on the floor, and upon seeing that it was a zombie, he walked up behind it and shot the evil undead clown in the back of the head. The face was blown out and the skull was forced back onto the floor. The hand that had reached out to grab the clown's leg belonged to another zombie clown, and the trooper spun around and shot that one in the head as well. Pete didn't see this, as the clown was still hidden in the doorway, but the hand did flap up and down before remaining still in the hallway.

"You okay?" the trooper asked Pete.

Pete nodded and forced out, "I…I'm fine, yeah, thanks."

"Don't think nothin' of it." He walked past Pete and then on to the next apartment, his job one of cleanup, making sure there was no one left after the initial sweep.

After a full minute, Pete shook himself and was able to move again. What the fuck had just happened? One thing he knew, he needed to go back to the bathroom and wipe his ass because from the way he felt down there, he'd definitely shit himself a little. Walking bowlegged so as not to squish the mess between his legs, he went back to the bathroom and got cleaned up.

When he was done Pete returned to the basement, taking a different route than through the hallway with the evil clown.

The last of the undead clowns in the basement were just being destroyed by the other troopers in the room when Pete returned. He moved close to Dodger so he could talk to the man without anyone else overhearing. "You asked me a question, earlier," Pete said flatly to Dodger.

"Yeah, I did…and?"

"You can count me in," Pete said. "I think it's time to get the fuck out of here."

"Good, glad to have you on board."

As more police and riot troops moved in behind them to begin with the final cleanup, Pete and Dodger left, their destination outside, where the night air was clean and the stench of death wasn't as pungent as inside the apartment building.

The decision had been made. They were going to run. But first they would need to steal a squad car and make it free of the blockade surrounding the apartment building, and would need to do so without any of the other police catching on to what they were doing. Desertion wasn't taken lightly, especially now when things were so critical and manpower was at an all time low, due to the authorities being spread so thin across the city and surrounding burrows.

Both men knew that running could prove easier said than done.

The side fire door to the apartment complex was locked, but a good kick by Pete had it flying open to smack the brick wall of the building with a loud *clang*.

Behind them, in the stairwell, three zombie clowns lay twitching with their chests and heads demolished by gunfire, their colorful wigs now matted with bone and brain matter.

When Pete and Dodger had descended the stairs leading to the exit, the three zombie clowns had been waiting, almost as if they were setting up an ambush. But the undead clowns were no match for the two well-armed troopers, and in seconds, the bodies were riddled with lead as they dropped to the bottom of the stairwell.

As the two men stepped outside into the dark night, the blockade was still in full swing. More than a dozen squad cars were scattered around the apartment building, yellow sawhorses set up to keep the small crowd of onlookers at bay. Both Pete and Dodger moved away from the building and into the heart of the blockade.

Chaos reigned as men and women were escorted from the scene, while off to the left the first body bags were being taken out of the building. More than one bag had dark stains on its surface, signifying the occupant hadn't gone down easy.

Dodger paused to watch as a specially-assigned group of troopers was making a funeral pyre with the bodies in the parking lot. Whatever was happening in Boston, it had come to the point when there was no time to bring the bodies in for burial; instead they would be burned right there in the rear parking lot of the building. Parked near the pyre, but not too close, sat a wood-paneled station wagon, a Datsun, a Dodge Dart and a white Charger, their owners probably dead or zombies.

The bodies were tossed one on top of the other like cordwood, the black body bags sliding against one another. More than one hadn't been bothered to be zipped up, and as the bags landed and slid, colorfully-attired arms and upper torsos fell out.

Pete stepped on something that squeaked and he looked down to see that it was a red nose that had come off its owner's face. He squeezed the nose once, then twice, hearing the soft sound, like a dog's chew toy. He tossed it away from him, where it bounced a few times and rolled into a crowd of people. Pete stopped walking when he saw Dodger wasn't with him, and as he turned and went to join the man, Pete also paused to watch the pyre being lit.

A man wearing a white protective suit was tossing gasoline onto the bodies, then he stepped back and nodded to another man, who lit a road flare, then tossed it onto the colorful corpses.

Like a match being struck, the pile of arms and legs began to burn, dark black smoke drifting up into the night sky to be lost in the darkness. The distinctive odor of burning flesh and plastic floated on the air, the latter due to the clowns' wigs, noses and large floppy shoes.

As the fire burned, more bodies were added, some merely dead, not zombies. These were the clowns who had tried to take on the SWAT team but had lost miserably. Dodger watched as a clown with pink hair and a red suit was tossed into the flames like he was trash.

It's all such a terrible waste, Dodger thought as he felt Pete's hand on his shoulder.

"Come on, man, we need to blow this scene," Pete said in a low voice, not wanting any of their fellow officers to hear him.

"Huh? Oh, yeah, sorry, Pete, I was just…"

"Yeah, man, I know. It's cool, let's get moving. You said we need to be at the police dock by nine, right?"

Dodger checked his watch. It was almost eight.

"Yeah, that's right. A little after nine. The pilot said he's picking up his girlfriend first at nine sharp, then he'd meet me at the police dock. But it wouldn't take him long to get there from the television station."

"Okay then, let's move, man," Pete said, then turned and walked away, this time Dodger was with him. "What's the plan?" Pete asked as he plodded beside Dodger.

"We need to snag one of these cars without anyone gettin' wise on what we're gonna do with it."

"Why, you think we'll be stopped?" Pete asked.

Dodger lit a cigarette with his lighter and shrugged his shoulders. He nodded to a few fellow cops as he glided through the crowd of police and other men of authority. Everywhere he looked, the spotlights set up to face the building showed men yelling and arguing, no one really having a handle on the situation.

"Maybe, I just want to be prepared for everything," Dodger said.

From behind them, a side door to the apartment building opened and a cry went up as more than a dozen undead clowns spilled out. Clouds from the tear gas drifted out of the top of the doorway and at first the zombies were hidden, their true appearance unseen by the nearby police. Each man assumed the zombies were just more of the occupants escaping, the tear gas driving them out of their homes, but when the first undead clown reached a cop and sank its teeth into the man's arm, chaos exploded as the police found themselves becoming inundated with the comical undead.

The zombie clowns were quickly inside the ranks of the officers and a cacophony of yells, screams and gunshots filled the air as the men tried to defend themselves. A trooper turned when a black clown, dead for more than a day, tried to take a bite out of his shoulder. Spinning, the cop fired wildly, his bullets spraying not only the clown, but three of his fellow troopers. The hapless troopers soaked up the gunfire as they dropped to the pavement, bleeding out from a dozen bullet wounds. Of course they didn't get the chance to bleed out, as no sooner did they hit the ground then the undead clowns were on them, tearing at their black, SWAT uniforms for the warm flesh beneath.

Another SWAT trooper used the butt of his rifle to crack a female clown zombie in the face, the butt flattening her nose and pulping her features into a bloody gruel that mixed with the pasty makeup she wore. As the dead woman stumbled backwards, the man flipped his rifle over and shot her five times in the chest. He knew the head was where he needed to aim to take her down for good, but in his panic he wasn't thinking, falling back on old rules of shooting human beings in the chest to take them down.

The dead clown stumbled backward and was tripped by another clown. As she fell to the ground, she attempted to roll over, and when she tried to get up, her head was suddenly flattened when a large boot crushed it like a melon.

Dodger pulled his now gore-and-brain-covered boot out of the fetid mess and looked for another target. Next to him, Pete's rifle was searching for a target of his own, but with his fellow officers so closely packed together, he didn't want to risk a shot.

"What do we do?" Pete asked Dodger, deferring to the thinner but far more competent man.

"Our jobs," Dodger replied and punched a Puerto Rican clown ghoul in the head when it came for him. As the clown fell back, Dodger shot it point blank in the head, the skull exploding into a dozen fragments as brain matter rained down, along with strands of yellow wig.

Pete, taking Dodger's lead, began moving closer to the undead clowns, shooting them from so close that they received powder burns on their pale and blue flesh, the dark holes showing the scorch marks.

A moaning old man clown with a blue afro came for Dodger. The trooper kicked out with the sole of his black boot, catching the clown in the chest. As the zombie stumbled backwards, Dodger fired a round that took the clown between the eyes. The pasty, slack-jawed face was destroyed and the back of the skull disintegrated as the body toppled backwards, the blue afro getting blown right off the head along with half of the skull.

Dodger was now moving in and out of the shifting bodies like a wraith, his revolver drawn in his right hand, his rifle in his left. Each time a figure popped up out of the shifting shadows of tear gas clouds and white light of the spotlights, he took it down without mercy.

Pete swung to his right and shot a zombie clown coming at him from out of the darkness. The round caught the zombie in the neck, and a second later another round followed the first. Both bullets tore through the muscle and tendons, taking the head almost completely off like a knife through butter. As the dead clown stumbled around with its head hanging on by a few scraps of flesh, its feet tripped and it tumbled chest first to the pavement, where blood seeped from the open cavity to pool across the ground.

All around Dodger, his fellow cops were doing the same, and when the smoke finally cleared, more than two dozen bodies were sprawled on the pavement, more than one still twitching.

Stepping through the carnage, Dodger stopped walking as he leered over a clown with a bad orange wig, who was feeding on a now, very dead cop. Without hesitation, he shot the undead clown in the head, and as the body dropped to the ground, the dead cop's eyes snapped open.

"Damn it," Dodger muttered as he turned and shot the cop dead once more, a black hole appearing in the man's forehead. Dodger had known the man personally, had met his wife and kids, and now he'd been the one to put the guy down for good. He wondered who would tell the man's family he was dead, first devoured by a zombie and then put down when he rose from the dead himself.

All around Dodger, the battle was dwindling as the SWAT troopers finished off the remaining undead clowns. As the dust settled, more than a half dozen troopers and cops were dead, their bodies twitching as they slowly began to revive.

Sporadic gunfire carried on the wind as the remaining zombies were put down for good. Pete walked up to Dodger, his eyes wide from the carnage. He knew a lot of the men now sprawled on the ground, their throats ripped out, faces peeled back like old bananas. "How the hell did this happen?" Pete said more to himself than Dodger, who didn't reply, but instead spit into the blood pooling at his feet, then raised his revolver, and shot another good cop in the head just as the man slowly rose to a sitting position after reviving.

"Come on, Pete, we still have work to do," Dodger said in a gruff voice.

Pete nodded curtly, his dark face covered with a sheen of sweat, his bulk heaving in his uniform. With five more troopers by their side, the two troopers strode through the death and gore to put the reanimating cops down once and for all.

Chapter 4

"Okay, let's get these poor bastards to the fire at the other end of the building!" an authoritative voice cried out. He wore a blue sport coat, a white shirt underneath, and had a thin mustache riding his upper lip. He was the commander in charge of this little shindig and he took it very seriously.

Another man with a fedora and wire-rimmed eye glasses was standing next to him. This man, a sergeant, had been with the captain when the gas had been applied, and he now added his voice to the proceedings, much as he had commented before on how Bobo and his people inside the apartment building were going to fight the police.

"Wait, you're not going to place our fallen men in that fire, too, are you?" the sergeant asked.

The captain sighed and shook his head, the decision he'd made weighing heavily on him.

"What choice do I have? We don't have time to gather the bodies, you know that. Headquarters said to just add the bodies to the fire and be done with it. The time for niceties is over, hell, this shit is out of control as it is."

"But the families of those men…" the other man said.

The captain did a chopping motion with his hand in front of the sergeant's face, ending the conversation.

"Damn it, don't you think I know this? You know, you telling me isn't going to change a damn thing but make me feel worse. There's no time for proper burials and autopsies. You know that as well as I do. It sucks, but that's the way it is. Now how about helping instead of commenting, huh? Don't be such an asshole."

"Yes, sir," the sergeant said and moved off to help coordinate the cleanup. More of Bobo's people were being herded out of the building as well as the clowns who had refused to leave voluntarily. Screaming children, women, and old men over sixty, all wearing colored attire, were the majority; most of the middle-aged clowns had been gunned down when SWAT had attacked the building. The tear gas had been the deciding victory, none of the clowns able to fend off the eye-and-throat-clogging gas.

As the bodies of the zombie clowns and dead cops alike were gathered, Pete and Dodger lent a hand. Neither man could just turn and leave their brothers behind, not like this. As the bodies were tossed into the back of a SWAT truck, both men felt their hearts fill with lead. The dead faces of their fellow brothers gazed back at them accusingly, many having only the bullet holes in their foreheads to tell of their violent deaths, though many had bloody wounds suffered by the hands and teeth of the undead clowns' violent attack.

As Dodger put another corpse down, he turned as two riot troopers carried another cop between them. Dodger stepped aside to let the men closer. The corpse's back was peppered from gunfire. Gunfire inflicted when the cop had been shot by a clown wielding an Uzi.

As Dodger watched the two troopers toss the corpse into the back of the truck, Pete stepped up next to him, just as Dodger lit a cigarette.

Pete had pulled out a cigarette of his own, a dark brown cigarette that smelt of cloves. As he popped it into his mouth, he found Dodger's lighter below his nose, the flame flickering in the night air. Without saying a word, Pete bent forward, lit his cigarette, and nodded curtly to his fellow trooper. Dodger said nothing, but only snapped the Zippo closed with a flick of his wrist and made it disappear into his black jumpsuit. His turtle neck was high on his neck and only his face and hands stood out in the shadows, the truck blocking most of the spotlights.

"This really sucks, man," Pete said while exhaling smoke from his lungs.

"Yeah, I know it sucks," Dodger said. "That's why we need to get outta here."

Pete exhaled another plume of smoke and stepped in front of Dodger. "So we going now?"

Dodger checked his wristwatch. "Yeah, it's already past eight. I told Kevin if I was gonna go with him I'd be there by nine. If I'm not there—if we're not there—he's gonna leave without us." Dodger glared at Pete, the cold eyes of a warrior within the dark orbs. "Okay, let's get moving."

Pete stepped aside to let Dodger go first, and the two headed off towards the squad cars lining the blockade, Pete having to move a little faster to keep up thanks to his large bulk. As they walked, they stepped on deflated and popped balloons, a residue of the battle between the clowns.

Both men knew they had done all they could for their fellow troopers and the city itself. Now it was time to worry about themselves and seek an escape route.

But the rendezvous was across the city, and there was no way of knowing what awaited them between there and where they were now.

Dodger and Pete worked their way through the crowd, their destination being the squad cars at the very outer perimeter of the police line. As they passed by a row of ambulances, Dodger slowed to watch two paramedics working on a black woman in a clown outfit, wearing a bloody yellow suit with bright white hair for a wig and the classic pancake makeup over her face. Her neck was a torn mess and the two men were struggling to get the bleeding under control, though it didn't look good. They were inside the ambulance.

Dodger stopped and began to move closer, Pete following, though he didn't understand where Dodger was going. If they were going to make a run for it then Dodger was going the wrong way.

Dodger watched the female clown as she lay prone on the gurney; she didn't look like she was going to make it.

Which was what he was waiting for.

Pete, though not understanding what Dodger was doing, stood beside his new friend anxiously, his eyes flicking about nervously as he waited for someone of authority to call out and ask what he and Dodger thought they were doing and where they were going.

"I'm losing her," the first paramedic said. "Give her a shot of adrenalin."

The second paramedic complied, but the woman didn't respond. Dodger saw her chest rise one last time as she inhaled her last breath, then she exhaled it, her eyelids fluttering once, her mouth going slack.

On a monitor in the ambulance, the white line went from a jumping beat to a flat line.

"That's it, she's gone," the first paramedic said calmly. He'd done all he could and death was a part of his job…as much as life was.

"Dodger, what the hell are we waiting for? We need to go."

Dodger lit another cigarette and stuffed his lighter away. "In a minute, Pete, just a minute more," he replied smoothly as his right hand calmly went to the revolver on his hip. All around the two troopers, screams, yells and sporadic gunfire could be heard, and so far no one was paying either Dodger or Pete the slightest bit of attention.

Pete was about to ask yet again, knowing to hang around was madness if they were truly going to leave, when the female clown on the gurney suddenly opened her eyes and uttered a guttural moan.

The two paramedics, still not used to their patients reviving after they'd died, were totally caught off guard, and the first man screamed as the undead clown reached out with her left hand and grabbed his arm, pulling his wrist towards her mouth so she could feed.

A sharp crack of Dodger's revolver filled the area surrounding the ambulance and the dead woman's forehead blossomed a red hole, half her skull blowing out to splatter onto the pillow on the gurney, along with her bright-white wig, now stained red. The body was slammed back down from the force of the heavy round and the hand let go of the paramedic.

Jumping away, the paramedic stared at the dead clown and her brains now dripping over the side of the gurney.

Dodger turned to casually look at Pete and said, "Now we can go."

Pete smirked slightly and the two troopers walked away, the pair of paramedics still staring at the now very dead clown, their eyes glancing out of the ambulance to see Dodger already leaving.

The paramedic who'd been saved didn't even get the chance to tell Dodger thank you before the two troopers were lost in the chaos of the blockade.

"So which one do we take?" Pete asked as he studied the five black and white squad cars lined up one next to the other at the edge of the blockade. The gumball lights on the car roofs were on, the red and blue strobes casting shadows in every direction. The street lights were out in this section of the city and only the vehicles' lights pushed back the night.

There were seven troopers on patrol near the cars, each moving about as they managed the crowd gathered nearby. Though most citizens were smart enough to stay indoors, not wanting to risk meeting one of the walking dead, there were still more than enough who feared nothing. Hookers, drug dealers and homeless people stood at the edge of the barricade, numbering more than thirty strong, all watching the apartment building be assaulted. They sent catcalls and derivatives at the police, taunting them with each word and insult.

The apartment building wasn't in the best part of town and the police normally were never seen unless someone was getting rousted. But this time the damn cops were rousting an entire apartment building!

"Doesn't matter, one's good as another," Dodger replied.

Pete was about to add a retort when he felt a hand fall onto his shoulder. Turning, he found himself looking into the face of the sergeant, the man doing rounds to see how the rest of the troopers were doing.

"What the hell are you doing over here?" the sergeant asked in an angry voice. "You're supposed to be inside sweeping the building with Mario's unit."

Then the gruff man turned to see Dodger standing behind him. "And you, I sure as hell know you're not supposed to be back here," he snapped at Dodger.

"Oh, uh, yeah, Sarge, about that," Dodger replied. "The captain told us to head over here and make sure there's no trouble on the police line. He figured maybe with everything going on that some of the bystanders might get antsy and try something. He said we should take a car and drive around the perimeter. You know, show a police presence."

"He did, huh? That don't sound right. Especially as we need more men on body duty." The man shook his head in disgust. "Christ, we have to burn our own damn men with those *things*, it ain't right I tell ya. Fucking clowns are an abomination." He reached down to his two-way radio on his belt. "I'm gonna check with the captain to make sure what you say is true."

Dodger and Pete looked at one another, their gazes locked. They knew what would happen if the sergeant got through to the captain. He'd find out that Dodger and Pete had abandoned their posts sweeping the inside of the building and were probably looking to desert. It was happening more and more as time passed and the situation grew worse. If a trooper was found deserting, they now received a lot more than a reprimand and a slap on the wrist.

The sergeant began calling his superior, but the captain wasn't answering. The sergeant tried twice more and finally gave up.

"Look, you two, I don't care what the captain said. Get your asses back to the building and help with disposal, that's an order." Without waiting for a reply, he turned and moved away to check on the rest of the men. Everyone was uneasy and the veteran of over twenty years knew one itchy trigger finger aimed at the unsettled crowd surrounding the barricade could cause a riot the police could never contain.

Pete looked at Dodger again as the sergeant receded into the night.

"Damn that was close," Pete sighed. He was hungry but knew he wouldn't be eating anything for a while.

"Too close," Dodger added.

"Once he catches up to the captain and asks him about us…" Pete let the rest hang.

"Yeah, so we better get moving," Dodger said as he moved towards the line of black and whites cars. Pete followed, having to pick up his steps again, thanks to his size making him slower than Dodger's quickened gait.

The other cops ignored Dodger and Pete, not knowing or caring what they might be doing on the edge of the barricade. There were so many people doing so many things no one person knew what everyone else was doing. This would be an opportunity for the two men, who were quickly able to find a squad car with the keys still in the ignition that wasn't blocked in too badly.

Many of the cops had been in a rush to arrive at the apartment building, and so had left the keys in the ignitions, as no one would have been stupid enough to steal the squad cars, the police figured. It took only a few minutes to find a squad car with the keys dangling from the steering column, and as they climbed in and the doors slammed closed, the cacophony of screams and gunshots dwindled within the interior of the vehicle. Dodger was in the driver's seat and he turned over the engine, then hit the siren.

As he slowly backed out of his spot, bystanders had to move out of his way, more than once sending a curse or flipping the two troopers off. Dodger hit the horn a few times as well to get the crowd to move faster, and a minute later the car was free of the crowd.

As Pete stared at the faces of the hookers and drug dealers who yelled at him and called him derogatory names through the window, the crowd parted. That was when he saw the sergeant running towards the squad car, waving a fist at him and Dodger.

"Uh, Dodger the sergeant is…" Pete said, trailing off again.

"Yeah, man, I see him," Dodger replied, but instead of stopping and waiting for the man to catch up, he swung the wheel and floored the gas pedal, the cruiser shooting out into the street.

"He looks pissed. He must've found out the captain doesn't know a thing about us," Pete said as the black and white shot down the dark street. A few shadowy forms lined the sidewalks, but it was mostly deserted. This area of town was full of rundown, dilapidated buildings, many in the same state of repair as the apartment they were leaving behind

"Why, you plan on comin' back here?" Dodger asked.

"No, guess not."

"Exactly, so what he thinks he knows doesn't mean shit. We pretty much just gave our resignations and this car is our severance package."

Pete grinned and Dodger pulled out his pack of smokes, sliding one out with his teeth. As he went to put the pack away and dig for his cigarette lighter, Pete held up a hand for Dodger to pause, then hit the one on the car's dashboard, and a few seconds later, he took it and raised it to Dodger's cigarette.

Dodger leaned forward and took the proffered light, then Pete pulled it back and slid it back into the dashboard. The two were already getting into a groove and they had only known each other for an hour.

As the squad car drove deeper into the city, all around them, Boston began to burn.

As the squad car cut through the heart of the city to reach the north side and the police dock at the marina, the moonlight cast its pallid glow on an embattled city. Destruction was everywhere, more than one dark shadow sprawled on the street being a corpse, and more than a few were walking around, like drunks after last call. Automatic gunfire and explosions filled the air as the squad car weaved through the stalled traffic.

It seemed like overnight, the city had collapsed and chaos reigned supreme.

Stalled and abandoned cars and trucks littered the road as Dodger swerved around and through the obstructions. Once the front tire ran over a severed hand and the sound of brittle bones carried into the interior.

Neither Dodger nor Pete commented on it, both wanting to pretend it didn't happen.

As they drove deeper into downtown, signs of looting were more apparent. Storefronts and convenience stores had shattered windows and sparking overhead lights, more than one showing telltale signs of violence.

There were more people, too—pedestrians running to or from something.

Dodger checked his watch to see it was coming on 8:30. Good, they still had plenty of time to reach the police dock and the waiting helicopter. Of course, there was always the possibility Kevin wouldn't be there, but he had been friends with Kevin for years, and if the pilot told him he would be there, then Dodger was confident the man would do everything in his power to do so.

"Wait, stop here, Stop!" Pete yelled and Dodger slammed on the brakes. Pete jumped out of the squad car, yelling, "I'll be right back."

"Where the fuck are you going?" Dodger called but Pete was too far away to hear through the glass of the closed passenger window. Dodger watched Pete run into a convenience store, pushing his large bulk through the hanging and smashed door that led into the dark store.

Dodger nervously tapped the steering wheel with his fingers, not liking where he was. He felt vulnerable, and as he gazed around the car, he saw shadows lurking in nearby alleyways.

A full three minutes passed, and Dodger was about to get out of the car and go after Pete when the bulky trooper appeared in the doorway again. He was running as fast as his oversized form would allow. In his hands he held a couple of large boxes over-flowing with sugary treats. As he ran, the boxes jiggled, and the sugary treats jumped out of the top box to fall onto the sidewalk. Pete ran to the squad car, opened the back door where perps would go, and tossed the boxes inside. They landed hard on the seat and fell over, their contents tumbling to the floor and across the seat. Dodger glanced back to see an assortment of Twinkies, Snowballs, Ho-Hos and cupcakes.

Movement at the store doorway caused Dodger to look up. Three zombies were stumbling through the door, their shoulders rubbing as they tried to exit at the same time. But then they popped through and were crossing the sidewalk to the squad car.

Pete jumped inside the car, his mouth already full of Twinkies and Ho-Hos. Cream filling coated his mouth like makeup and Dodger had a flashback to the undead clowns. Shaking off the chill he felt, he snapped at Pete, "What the hell, man? You stopped for baked goods?"

"I was hungry," Pete said like a chastised child. "Starving actually, and who knows when I'll get to eat again?" He shrugged. "And who knows if there'll ever be Twinkies and Ho-Hos again?"

"Oh please, there'll always be Twinkies and cupcakes," Dodger replied as he put the transmission into gear and began to drive. The three zombies slapped the side of the car ineffectually.

"Nah-ah," Pete said around a mouthful of a Snowball. "Something could happen. A strike maybe, or the company could go bankrupt."

"Please," Dodger scoffed. "The guys who run Hostess would have to be pretty damn incompetent to let the place go to hell and let that happen. So if we're gonna make up shit, how 'bout the airlines or the big three car companies. Are they gonna go bankrupt, too?"

"They could," Pete said but he didn't sound so sure of himself. GM and the other big car companies made money by the bucket loads. There would be no way for them to ever go bankrupt. The same went to the people who made Twinkies.

"No, man, they couldn't," Dodger said. "It's too far-fetched. It's 1979, man, the world is in great shape. Once this zombie thing is taken care of everything'll go back to normal."

"You really think that, Dodger?"

"Of course I do," Dodger replied, saying it as much for Pete as himself. The dead couldn't take down all of civilization, it was ridiculous, or as much as Hostess going bankrupt anyway.

Pete was pouting and Dodger glanced at him. "What's wrong now?"

"They're not *cupcakes*, they're called Ho-Hos," Pete said, a connoisseur of the tasty treats.

Dodger blinked at this, as if to say, 'really?' but he said nothing, looking back to the road. To maneuver around a particularly nasty accident—the three cars now just crushed metal with blood on the windows and windshields—Dodger had to slow the car to a crawl. As he did so, a shrieking man suddenly came running out of a side alley, bounced off the driver's door, and began to pound on Dodger's window. He was half-naked, his clothing looking like it had been torn off his body; there were large scratches on his face and neck as well.

Dodger's immediate instinct was that the man had run afoul of a few of the walking dead, but as soon as he began screaming for help, five women came charging out of the alley. The woman in the lead was carrying what was obviously the man's underwear.

"Get back here, you prick! We're not done with you yet!" the first woman screamed. When she saw the black and white squad car, she swore angrily. "Shit, cops!" But then she realized there were only two cops and there were five of them, and they were all armed. If she seemed intimidated by the two troopers, she showed none of it.

Inside the patrol car, Dodger looked past the half-naked man banging on his window, leaving red streaks on the glass, and took in the five women who had come out of the alley. They all wore sharp business suits and high heels. They looked like they had come from work; only instead of going home they had decided to rape a man. Mob mentality at its worst, Dodger figured. People did the worst things when they thought there was no law to enforce the rules, and even women could fall to their baser instincts.

All five women were armed; three holding small handguns and two had what looked like sawed-off shotguns. Dodger knew in the confines of an alley or the inside of a building, the sawed-offs would be devastating to anyone unfortunate enough to be standing in front of the blast. He idly wondered where the women had gotten the weapons, but quickly decided it didn't matter. They had them, that was what mattered.

It was as Dodger was watching the women that he saw the leader, the one holding the man's underwear, bring up her shotgun and level it at the man and also the squad car.

"Get down!" Dodger yelled, reaching out to Pete and pushing the fat man lower in the seat just as the massive report of the weapon reverberated across the area.

Both troopers felt the impact of the blast against the driver's side of the squad car, but nothing happened other than a muffled thump.

Neither man understood this until Dodger risked a peek to see what was happening. The half-naked man was still feebly banging on the side of the squad car, but as Dodger stared using the side-view mirror, he saw the guy's lower half was now gone, severed by the barrage from the shotgun.

As the man's intestines slid out of his body to splash onto the pavement, his legs lying in the road like two spent logs, his mouth opened and closed and his one free hand continued to slap the window. The other hand was holding the top edge of the roof of the car, keeping him attached to the side. Dodger could only stare in horror as the man's grip grew weak and his grasp failed him, the body falling away to twitch next to the squad car and lower half.

"You guys *suuuuckkkk*," he whispered as he slid down the car.

Dodger had less than a second to take in the brutality of the man's death before more gunshots filled the street, and he knew he needed to act fast.

"What the fuck is going on?" Pete yelled as bullets slapped the side of the squad car.

"Looks like a gang was raping him! Damn it, we need to get out of here!" Dodger snapped as he tried to steer around the three car crash blocking the road. He slammed the transmission into reverse, but no sooner did he do this than the right rear tire was blown out by a stray bullet. He ignored this, not worried about driving on the rim, but as he tried to back up, Dodger found he couldn't. With the tire flat, he couldn't get the traction he needed, as that was the tire that moved the vehicle.

As bullets pounded the car, Dodger pushed Pete against the passenger door.

"Get out, you fat fuck! We need to return fire or we're both dead!" Dodger yelled.

Pete wasn't a trained warrior, so he never even thought about questioning Dodger's assessment. Reaching out, he pulled the handle on the door, and as it flew open, Pete jumped out and went to his knees, Dodger following right behind him.

Both men went to either side of the car, Dodger going to the hood and Pete the trunk, thanks to Dodger pointing and directing the black man, and though they weren't a well-oiled team, they did begin to return fire, giving back a little of what they were receiving.

"We're pretty well fucked here, you know that, right?" Dodger yelled out to Pete, who only nodded.

They continued to shoot as the five women began to spread out and surround them.

Chapter 5

As Dodger and Pete crouched behind the squad car, the chilling fact that they couldn't call for backup weighed heavily on them both. By now, the sergeant would have put the word out on the two-way that two of his men had stolen a squad car and were deserting the force, and he'd be damned if he would let them get away with it.

Dodger had his rifle in his hands, while Pete held his revolver. Dodger was the first to return fire, and as he lined up and fired over the trunk, one of the women went flying backwards, the bullet shredding her heart. She fell onto her back, her legs going up into the air, her panties showing for all to see. Dodger had the briefest view of pink ones before her legs dropped back down and she lay still.

Pete was next to lay a woman out. He lined up a shot, but the first bullet went wild, due to his shaking hand. He wasn't built for battle and it was all he could do not to get up and run away. "Shit," he spit as he realigned his target. "I can do this, I know I can."

The second round caught a red-headed woman in a gray power suit in the upper right shoulder. The woman was sent backwards to fall onto the sidewalk, where Pete then put her down for good with a shot to the chest. The woman's left high heel shoe flew off as she fell, to spin in the air before sailing back to earth.

That left three females to go, and Dodger was next to score a hit. As bullets whined around his head, he calmly shot a woman in the stomach, the gut shot dropping her face first to the pavement with a ragged, bloody wound where her belly button used to be. She mumbled something about how it was a bitch to get blood out of cotton, then toppled to the ground.

Pete had to duck behind the squad car as a barrage of shotgun blasts soared over his head, the pellets scarring the paint of the black and white car. The side of the vehicle looked like it had been through a sandstorm and been buried for years before driving back into the city. When the barrage finally stopped, and the woman began trying to reload, Pete stood up and shot her in the neck, severing her jugular and sending her flying backwards. As she landed on the pavement, her blood spread out in a growing pool of dark liquid as she gasped for breath, but only managed to suck in blood. Drowning, the fourth woman spasmed as her eyes fluttered their last.

"Take that, you psycho bitch!" Pete yelled as he admired his marksmanship.

That left the leader, a middle-aged, heavy-set Spanish woman with a thin mustache, muscular arms, and a large bushy hairdo. She yelled in anger to see her fellow females gunned down so easily, and she shot at Pete and Dodger, spraying the entire squad car with buckshot. The shotgun was easy for her to wield, given her thick stature. But she was a little too far away and the sawed-off lost much of its punch by the time the blast reached the car.

Dodger, waiting for the right moment, popped up and shot the woman in the shoulder. She was knocked backwards, and where her back met the building that made up the wall of the left side of the alley, she left a dark-red blood stain behind. Cursing a blue streak, the wounded woman turned and fled down the alleyway, her running form swallowed by the darkness.

Dodger never hesitated when he saw her turn and flee. He jumped up and dashed for the alley, his rifle in his hands, as he ran as fast as his legs would allow.

"Dodger! Where the hell are you going?" Pete called out, not understanding where his partner was going.

"To finish this!" he yelled back, his voice hard and cold.

From where Pete had been sitting in the squad car earlier, the black trooper hadn't seen the man cut in half by the shotgun blast when they'd first arrived, but Dodger had, and though Dodger knew they needed to get to the police dock, his honor wouldn't let the bitch get away with cold-blooded murder, especially when he was a witness to it. He was still a cop and he took the oath to serve and protect seriously.

"Shit!" Pete yelled, but he took off after his partner, his chubby legs making him waddle. He might not agree with the choice Dodger had made, but he wouldn't leave him alone. As Pete charged across the street and into the dark alleyway, jumping over the prone bodies, and almost not clearing them due to his weight, he glanced down at the dead women, the four corpses still leaking blood onto the ground.

As Pete ran, he checked his watch, the dials glowing softly, and he saw it was getting late. The time to reach the police dock was growing short. Shaking his head, he put on a burst of speed. *Man, we're cutting it close,* he thought as his eyes searched every shadow of the alley.

There was a muzzle flash up ahead at the far end of the alley, and Pete ducked behind a dumpster, the smell of urine and decay filtering into his sinuses. Boston was a beautiful city, but it had its hidden underbelly, where crime and disease was rampant. Unfortunately, the alleyways and hidden doorways were where a lot of that seediness was prevalent.

He heard Dodger's rifle fire twice and then another blast of the shotgun from the woman he was chasing. He waited until it looked safe, then began moving from trashcan to dumpster to a pile of old wooden pallets.

His partner was somewhere at the end of the alley and he needed to reach him.

Dodger ducked down behind a filthy green dumpster as a barrage of buckshot flew by him, the patter of the pellets so strong it felt like the dumpster actually moved an inch on its wheels when the blast struck it. When the woman fired, the alley lit up like a car's high beams had been turned on, and Dodger made sure to look away or risk losing his night sight. It was almost pitch black in the alley, the dull moonlight not able to penetrate past the buildings on either side. Gritting his teeth and setting his jaw taut, he waited for his chance to end this.

"Come on, you bastard! I'll take your ass down! You fuck, you killed all my girlfriends!" the woman screamed as she cracked open the housing to her shotgun, slid two more shells into the chamber, then flicked the short barrel up and closed the breach.

"Shit, why couldn't they have been normal woman, talking about bake sales and the like?" he murmured. "I had to get the ones that want to take back the night or some shit for equality." Dodger didn't move from behind the dumpster and the woman continued screaming curses. Dodger knew the woman's shoulder was bleeding profusely, but either she was on something or she was so full of rage that she didn't feel pain.

Maybe it's that time of the month, he thought with a sneer.

The woman fired again, the lead pellets flying down the middle of the alleyway.

Dodger waited for the initial blast and light, then he jumped out, rolled across the filthy ground, and came up a few feet closer to his target.

If he was correct, the woman hadn't seen him change position. Slowly, praying he wasn't about to get his head shot off, Dodger poked his right eye around the new dumpster he was hiding behind. This one had the redolence of Chinese food, while the other had smelled like rotten lettuce.

When he had a clear view of the alley, he could see the woman's body silhouetted at the opposite end of the alley. The foolish bitch didn't realize she was making herself a perfect target, as she wasn't thinking of defense, only offense.

Dodger waited for the woman to fire again and ducked back slightly as the barrage peppered the dumpster he'd been behind a second ago. Upon seeing that the woman didn't know where he was, Dodger brought up his rifle and set it on the new dumpster, placing his eye to the scope. He was a crack shot and all he needed was a few seconds to line up his target.

As the scope moved slightly, the woman's head came into focus, though it was a darker blob amongst others. Dodger let out his breath slowly, and as he gently inhaled, then exhaled, he squeezed the trigger.

Through the scope, he saw the woman throw her hands up as she went toppling backwards. As the woman fell over, Dodger stepped out, his rifle now leveled at waist height, his finger still on the trigger.

He heard heavy, thudding footsteps behind him, and when he turned, he saw Pete materialize out of the darkness, wheezing like a locomotive.

"You okay?" the black trooper asked. He was winded to the point of falling over, his face covered in a sheen of perspiration.

"You need to cut down on the Twinkies, pal," Dodger said with a grin.

"Tell me about it." He gestured to the end of the alley. "She dead?"

"Yeah, I got her. What took you so long?" Dodger joked, smiling wanly, knowing exactly what had taken Pete so long.

"Yeah, yeah, I'm not in the best of shape. I get it, can we move on now?" Pete asked.

"Sure, pal. I'm gonna go check her out, make sure she's down for good. Watch my back." Dodger then headed up the alley.

Pete, his revolver in hand, nodded once, then slowly followed while his eyes still searched the shadows. He was breathing easier now, too. He spotted movement once, and when he swiveled to the side, his finger a quarter ounce from firing, he stopped at the last instant, seeing two furry rats crawl out from under some dirty cardboard as they made their way to the next pile of refuse. Feeling silly, he moved further down the alleyway to catch up with Dodger.

The trooper was standing over the supine woman, half her skull splattered behind her, bits of brain matter looking like pink, shell-less snails in the moonlight.

When Pete reached Dodger, he too gazed down at the dead woman. Pete saw that the dead woman's left eye was gone, a large open wound now replacing the orb. This was the entry point of Dodger's bullet, an excellent shot considering the lighting and distance, not to mention the time he had to line up the shot.

"Nice," was all Pete could think to say.

"Yeah. The bitch got what she deserved." Dodger checked his watch again to see it was now a quarter to nine. "Pete, we're running out of time. Kevin said he wouldn't wait around for me and I told him that was fine. I said if I wasn't there at nine sharp then I wasn't coming. Granted we probably have a few extra minutes, but if he's ahead of schedule we're sunk."

There was movement down the right side of the street as the two troopers glanced left and right at the end of the alley. They both looked at the same time to see what seemed to be ten people walking down the street rather slowly. At first they appeared ordinary, though they were all moving in a way that didn't look quite right, and when the first few wandered under a working streetlight, it was clear to both troopers that these weren't people any longer, but were the walking dead.

Then the first zombies in line spotted Dodger and Pete and began walking in their direction, the faces now taking on something that looked a lot like true interest. But they were still at the end of the street and it would take the undead crowd a while to reach the two SWAT troopers.

"Shit, there's some more of 'em?" Pete said solemnly while wiping his brow with the back of his arm, gesturing to the left side of the street, where more zombies had appeared.

"Probably; they can't contain this, that's for sure. It's getting worse by the hour," Dodger said. "Let's get out of here. I did what needed to be done."

Pete said nothing, but only turned and began walking back into the alleyway.

Dodger looked over his shoulder one last time at the approaching zombies and then, he too, followed his new partner.

Minutes later, the first zombies reached the dead woman, and like children fighting over a fallen piñata, they went to their knees and began tearing at the still-warm corpse. Clawed hands dug into the soft flesh of the woman's stomach, tearing and pulling until the skin was flayed from the bone. The rib cage was soon cracked and hands dug deep, pulling out the warm insides, feeding on the spleen, kidney and liver. Entrails were pulled out like a magician's magic trick, one zombie taking a greasy rope of intestine and walking away, the multiple feet of glistening rope dragging out behind it until another zombie stepped on the crimson cord and caused it to rip.

The zombie was yanked back like a dog that had reached the end of its leash, but the zombie only yanked harder and the intestine came free. Ignorant on what had happened, the zombie stumbled onward, chewing on the intestine like it was a massive, raw sausage link. Congealing blood spilled out to coat the cement red as greedy mouths dropped to the ground to lap it up like puppies to milk.

In less time than it took to kill the woman, the zombies had torn her apart until there was nothing left but a bloody carcass that vaguely resembled a human torso, all the limbs and the head now gone.

With their chunks of flesh and entrails, the zombies moved off, eating on the move as they stuffed their mouths and filled their stomachs with human flesh.

When the last one was gone, the rats in the alley appeared, and soon were covering the corpse, feeding on what little remained.

The zombies had been thorough, and anything worth eating was now long gone. But the rats wouldn't complain; they would find what was left, the small bits and pieces, ignorant of the origin of the meat, and just glad to have sustenance.

At a steady jog, Dodger reached the opposite end of the alley where the squad car waited, the run taking him less than fifteen seconds. Turning, he frowned as he waited for Pete to catch up, the fat trooper wheezing and blowing out air as he did his best to keep up.

"Seriously, Pete, lay off the fucking Twinkies," Dodger said when Pete finally reached him.

"I'll go on a diet tomorrow. I promise," Pete replied as he leaned against the alley wall and recovered his breath.

In the time the two troopers had been gone, the situation at the mouth of the alley had changed drastically. The gunned-down women were no longer on the ground surrounded by pools of blood. Now, they were standing again, and were feeding on the man who had been shot in half by the first woman.

There were also three more zombies added to the four females, to make a total of seven. The three new zombies had heard the sounds of the gun battle and had stumbled towards the alley and the squad car, arriving just as Dodger and Pete had disappeared into the alley in pursuit of the lead woman.

As Dodger and Pete slowed to a stop, gripping their weapons tightly, they stared at the feeding zombies as they chowed down on the dead man's entrails and internal organs.

But as soon as the zombies began feasting, the dead man's eyes snapped open. Vacant eyes looked around, and he slapped a nearby zombie in the face, his hand waving around as if it had a mind of its own.

As the zombies lost interest in his reanimated flesh, the half-man used his arms to begin crawling away, dragging himself across the road as his intestines splayed out behind him. He ended up pulling himself under the squad car, his sense of direction off. But the rest of the zombies still wanted meat, and they tore at his severed waist and legs, tearing the fatty tissue off the thighs and calves.

The two troopers stared in disgust, fascination, and more than a little fear, though it festered deep in their guts like acid.

"When Hell is full, the dead will rise..." Dodger whispered softly; so low Pete didn't hear what he said over the feeding frenzy and moaning twenty feet away.

"What's that, Dodger?" Pete asked.

"Huh? Nothing, Pete, just thought of something I heard once. I'll tell you later if I get a chance."

They had no choice on what to do next; they had to take down the zombies so they could reach the squad car; it was too risky to just try and run for it. The time it would take to open the doors could spell their deaths.

Dodger aimed his rifle at the seven zombies, then slapped Pete on the shoulder. "Come, on, man, let's get this done and get goin'."

Pete nodded and raised his revolver. His rifle was still in the squad car. In all the excitement of escaping the vehicle, he hadn't grabbed it. He flicked open the wheel cylinder of his gun to see he had only a few rounds left. "I'm low on ammo and my extra bullets are in my belt on the front seat," he told Dodger.

Dodger checked his ammunition and then shook his head. "Shit, I'm low, too. Okay, let me take point and you bat cleanup. There's only seven of 'em. We can do this easy."

Pete blinked his reply, his visage saying he was on board, though he'd rather not be. The zombies had now turned to face the two troopers, having lost interest in the severed man's lower half. They began to shuffle towards the two men.

Though it would have been quite easy to turn and run away, outdistancing the zombies, the two troopers needed to get back to the squad car as fast as possible so they only had the one option, and there was no time for games such as leading the dead away to double back later.

Around or through, those were the choices. But as the zombies spread out, the only way was through. Dodger raised his rifle to his shoulder, lining up the first pale face in his sights. Then he fired, blowing out the rear skull of the undead woman. The body was thrown backwards to strike another woman who was knocked off balance, but soon righted herself.

Dodger shifted his aim and shot another one, this one the woman who had been shot in the throat. Bright arterial blood glistened in the moonlight, the entire front of her body covered in scarlet from bleeding out.

This time Pete's bullet hit the zombie in the nose, shattering cartilage as the round continued into the brain to then take out the rear skull plate. *Two down, five to go,* Pete thought while shifting his aim. He took a shot despite being low on bullets and another woman went down with an exploded eye and half a head. The body flopped to the pavement like a landed fish as the arms spasmed in death.

"Nice shot, man," Dodger commented as he lined up another target.

Pete beamed with pride. He already felt a kinship with Dodger, the man's strength and competency both admirable qualities, and he found himself wanting to impress Dodger desperately. The fact that Dodger seemed to accept Pete for who he was, obese and all, was another thing that endeared the fat man to Dodger.

The next target for Dodger was a mailman by the uniform the dead man wore, the zombie's throat all but ripped out right where the Adam's apple should have been. The mailman opened his mouth wide and moaned as he stumbled toward Dodger, and when the man was no more than eight feet away, Dodger fired, the round going into the mailman's mouth. Front teeth were blown away, shards of enamel flying up into the brain and out the sides of the pale cheeks.

The bullet continued on to sever the brainstem, the mailman flopping forward onto his face to twitch and spasm. The head was still active but the brain wasn't connected to the body any more.

The zombie was out of action for good; his days of delivering mail long over anyway.

One of the dead women was moving to the side of Dodger, but the trooper hadn't noticed this, the shadows on the street causing forms to blend together.

As she came up and prepared to sink her teeth into Dodger's arm, another gunshot rang out and the woman was thrown to the side, a large hole appearing in her chest. It wasn't a killing shot, but it saved Dodger, who swiveled at the waist and shot the woman at point blank range. The head didn't just explode, it disintegrated from the high impact of the bullet, sending skull fragments skittering across the road like a flat rock on the smooth surface of a lake.

Dodger turned to Pete and gave him a curt nod in thanks. "Thanks, man, I missed that one."

"Anytime," Pete grinned, then turned and shot a waitress in the throat. His aim was off, however, and though the left side of her neck erupted in blood, she only paused before continuing on. Pete lined up another shot to finish off the woman, but the hammer clicked on a dead cylinder. "Shit, I'm out," he grunted as Dodger swiveled and prepared to shoot the waitress.

"I got her," Dodger said as if he was casually shooting cans with some buddies in the middle of a glade in the woods. The report of the gunshot reverberated throughout the street, as the waitress dropped with half her face missing.

Low moans carried on the wind and both troopers looked to their right, behind the squad car, to see more shuffling figures approaching.

"Oh great, even more of 'em," Pete stated.

"It doesn't matter, we're out of here, come on," Dodger said and strode toward the last zombie and the waiting squad car beyond. The zombie had once been a business man, complete with an expensive suit and shoes. Now the suit was covered in gore, the dark-maroon stain on his chest showing where his blood had seeped out of his wounds on his face and neck to slather him in blood. On his right wrist was a gold watch, probably worth more than what Dodger made in a year, but now it was junk, as the zombie could no longer tell time.

As Dodger took the lead, he decided to save a bullet, and as he reached the business man, he swung the butt of his rifle up and under the zombie's chin.

The loud *crack* filled the street and the dead man went flying backwards, his jaw now shattered. Falling to the pavement, the business man spit teeth and blood as the two troopers moved on, not caring if the zombie was down for good or not.

Pete waddled around the squad car and jumped into the passenger seat again while Dodger moved for the driver's door. But when he was about to open the door, a hand shot out from under the car and grabbed his left ankle.

He looked down quickly to see the eyes of the severed man who had been begging for help minutes ago glaring up at him. He didn't look the same as before however. Because the dead women had gotten to him and began feeding before he revived, the guy now had large portions of his face, arms and neck missing. His eyes, once a dark blue, were now bulging out of his bright-red skull, the visage resembling the orbs in a toy skull, where the eyes would flick back and forth, as the mouth gaped open and clicked.

Drawing his revolver, Dodger aimed it at the guy's head, wanting to put him out of his misery, forgetting he had no bullets left. Pete reached over and opened the driver's door a crack from inside the car to help Dodger along.

"Dodger, man, what's taking so long, we need to go!" Pete called.

That shook Dodger from his fugue state and he shook his head to clear it. Deciding there was no reason to shoot the zombie, he kicked out with his boot, hitting the man in the face. The half-zombie was pushed back under the squad car, and with Dodger free, he opened the door the rest of the way and climbed in, slamming the door closed as he slid behind the steering wheel.

"What was that about?" Pete inquired as he stared at Dodger, seeing something different in the trooper's expression compared to only a second ago. There was now a darker brooding aspect that though always there, sometimes came out stronger than other times.

"It's nothing, man, we're cool." Dodger turned over the engine and shifted the transmission into 'drive,' then drove off.

As the squad car began to move, rocking slightly due to the flat tire, there was a heavier bump under the left back tire, like a speed bump.

Pete turned his head slightly to look at Dodger, wondering if the man knew what he'd run over, but the brooding trooper said nothing, his eyes focused on the road ahead. Because of the flat tire, the steering was harder to control.

Dodger checked his watch. It was ten to nine. They still had time, only barely, to reach the police dock and hopefully, their transportation to escape a dying city.

Behind the squad car, the crushed skull of the bifurcated zombie spread out onto the pavement, the hands still twitching as the nerve endings finally ceased.

Overhead, the moon stood watch over the death and carnage, the only remaining witness to what had occurred.

The next twelve minutes were a tenuous thing as Dodger drove through the streets of downtown Boston. At the first possible chance he had, Dodger pulled over and quickly changed the flat. Luckily, the spare tire in the trunk was good and with Dodger working fast and Pete watching his back, they had the tire changed in four minutes flat. Dodger barely tightened the lug nuts before they were moving again, leaving the jack, the flat tire, and tire wrench behind. The new tire only had to stay on for a few miles and then it wouldn't matter.

At each intersection Dodger and Pete both kept waiting to get to the one crash or pile-up that wouldn't allow them to make it through. A few times Dodger had to double back and try a different route and then, only just, were they able to make it.

All around them the city was in chaos, people running about while others were looking to loot what they could from the shops and stores.

"Why are they out here like this?" Pete asked incredulously. "They were told to stay indoors."

Dodger shook his head slightly. "Yeah, but then the police changed that and told people to get to rescue stations, remember? Only thing, those damn stations are probably as bad or worse than if the people had stayed in their homes." He swung the car around a stalled panel truck and continued forward. The police dock was a few minutes away, and as he turned a final left, he reached the edge of the city and the road that would lead to the nearby marina.

"You were right to want to run," Pete said. "It's the only chance we've got. We stay here and we're all dead for sure."

"Yeah, that's what I figured," Dodger replied. He glanced at Pete. "Glad you're along for the ride, buddy, I can use the backup."

"Oh, yeah? What about this friend of yours…Kevin? Can't he do that for you?"

Dodger smirked, thinking of his friend. "You'd think so, but no. Kevin is a good helicopter pilot, took to it like it was nothing, but he's not that good with a gun. I took him to the range once."

He shook his head thinking about Kevin's abysmal score. "Let's say he's at his best when he's flying, and he's new to that, too."

Pete actually grinned then. It was nice having a friend. Being so fat all of his life, making friends had been hard, and in high school all anyone did was make fun of him. "I hear ya, man." Pete gestured with his chin to the road ahead of them. "It looks like we're almost there."

Dodger looked forward again to see they were on an open road that wound around the coast to bring them to the marina.

Thank God! Dodger thought as the squad car drew closer to its destination. There was the traffic copter sitting on the police dock, its running lights blinking as it sat under the one lamp post that illuminated the dock and its single gas pump. Other than that, he couldn't see a thing, the darkness complete. Dodger stepped on the gas pedal harder now that he was finally clear of the city, and two minutes later, the car had reached the police dock.

"There's somethin' goin' on," Dodger said suspiciously as he put the black and white in park and grabbed his gear, Pete doing the same. Dodger left the keys in the ignition, figuring maybe some other poor bastard could use the squad car. He knew he wouldn't be needing it again. "They look like cops, too. Good, there's Kevin over in that corner," Dodger said.

Pete looked harder and he could see a man that was Kevin with a black leather jacket and short brown hair. He'd been pushed into a corner, one of the cops holding him there. But if the cop was interrogating Kevin or just trying to grab a ride was unknown at this time.

"Pete, let me handle this," Dodger said as he slung his rifle over his shoulder, closed the passenger door to the squad car, and casually walked the few feet to the dock so he was closer to the cop and Kevin. He saw there were a few other men on the dock, too, all wearing police uniforms.

"What's going on here?" Dodger asked politely, though his hand was hovering over the grip of his revolver. In the ride over, he'd reloaded and was now ready for whatever would come next.

"I caught your friend here stealin' fuel," the cop said, a bandolier filled with bullets covering his chest and wearing large handguns that weren't police issue on his hips. The cop had bright red hair and freckles, his eyes a dark blue.

"Friend?" Dodger said innocently.

"They know what I was doing and why, Dodger," Kevin said hesitantly, figuring there was no reason for the charade to go on any longer.

"Listen, no one should be shooting at anyone," the redheaded cop with the bandolier proposed. "We're all cops here after all; we're on the same side. It doesn't help any of us to get into a firefight, not when there's pusbags all over the place."

"I couldn't agree with you more," Dodger said. "How 'bout we have a truce?"

The cop shrugged. "Works for me." He took a step back from Kevin, who slinked away to join Dodger.

The other cops were gathering crates and supplies and were loading them into a small police launch. They had barely taken notice of the altercation that had just occurred.

"They're running, too, I guess," Pete said as he joined Dodger, pretty much stating the obvious.

"Fuck yeah, we're runnin'," the redheaded cop said. "We're gonna try for an island or someplace isolated? Fuck, anywhere's gotta be better than Beantown right now. Someplace we can go and hole up till all this shit is over."

"Where are you trying for exactly?" Kevin asked.

The cop shrugged. "Fuck if I know, pal. Any place will do, as long as those dead fucks aren't on it it'll be good as far as I'm concerned."

"You know, pal, you look familiar, have I seen you around before?" Dodger asked the man.

"Maybe, I get around a lot," was the reply. Then with a wave, the cop joined his buddies, the boat about ready to leave the dock, while the men argued and fought, one man asking if anyone had cigars with them. Another pulled out a pipe and handed it to the cop who wanted cigars; he slapped it away and snapped at his pal. "What the fuck am I gonna do with a pipe?" he asked as they all began talking at once.

While Kevin was getting ready to go in the helicopter, Dodger and Pete went back to the squad car to retrieve the rest of their gear. Dodger noticed that from a distance and from the front, it wasn't obvious that the squad car had been in a firefight. All the bullet holes were on the driver's side and the trunk.

With their supplies in hand, the two troopers headed back to the helicopter. Once there, Dodger spotted Pam and he glared at her—so Kevin had talked her into coming. In all the excitement since arriving, Dodger hadn't had time to say anything to her, as she'd waited silently in the helicopter. He wasn't a big fan of hers, thinking she was more than a little bit of a bitch, but Kevin liked her and that was good enough for Dodger. Hell, it wasn't like Dodger was dating her.

She glared back at him as Dodger climbed into the front passenger seat of the helicopter, leaving the back seat for Pete, who stowed his gear in the small compartment in the bottom of the helicopter, just above the landing skids. Then he climbed in next to Pam, his large bulk taking up almost all the room. Pam frowned at this, but said nothing.

"Who's the fat guy?" Kevin asked Dodger as he gestured to Pete, who was now loading his box of pastries and other gear into an even smaller compartment in the back of the helicopter right behind the rear seat.

"A friend," Dodger said, as if that was enough of an answer.

"He's pretty big. I hope the engine can carry all this extra weight," Kevin said as he started the engine, the rotor blades beginning to spin while he prepared for lift off.

"I'm sure you can manage it," Dodger replied, but before Kevin could respond, the sound of someone yelling suddenly broke through the din of the whirling blades.

"Wait, wait for me! Please take me with you!"

"Another friend of yours?" Kevin asked as everyone looked out the clear glass bubble of the chopper at the man running towards them.

"Never seen him before in my life," Dodger said.

While Kevin warmed up the engine, everyone watched the man as he raced towards the helicopter.

"I think he's being followed," Pam said from the backseat.

Dodger peered through the glass, trying to see behind the man. "Yeah, it looks like a mob of some kind."

The moon broke free from behind a patch of clouds then, illuminating the area around the dock a little better. That was when Dodger realized the crowd following the running man wasn't acting like normal people would. That was when he figured it out. "Shit, those people after that guy are zombies!"

"Great, even more of them," Pete said nervously.

The man reached the helicopter and he began banging on the window where Pam was sitting. "Please let me in. They're gonna get me! I don't want to die!"

The man was wearing a business suit, though the tie was loosened. His black shoes were scuffed, but it was easy to see that they had once been polished to a mirror finish.

Kevin began lifting off and Pam, seeing the man's face only inches before her, suddenly opened the door, allowing the man to jump in.

"Pam! What the fuck are you doing?" Kevin yelled. "We can't take him; we'll be too heavy to lift off!"

"Oh God, thank you, thank you for letting me in," the man wept as he climbed over Pam's lap and squeezed in between her and Pete.

"Well, I couldn't just sit here and watch him die as we flew away," she said. "I'm not that much of a bitch."

"Yeah, but you're close," Dodger added, Pam flipping him off and making a puss on her face,

"Well, you're generous act might end up getting us all killed," Kevin said as he began trying to get the chopper off the ground, the engine whining as he pushed on the throttle.

"Let it go, Kevin," Dodger said. "The guy's inside so you might as well accept it." Dodger glared at Pam, not happy with what she'd done. The first thing he'd come to realize since the crisis began was that you couldn't save everyone.

The man sobbed softly, his eyes wide in fear. He was a small man, with a thin face. A weasel came to mind, as Dodger stared at the man. He looked like a weasel, or a rat maybe. "What do you do for a living, pal?" Dodger asked the man.

"Why…why does it matter?" the man asked.

"No reason, just curious."

"I…I'm a lawyer," the man said through sobs.

"Uh-huh, there's a surprise," Dodger snapped. "Thanks, Pam," he said angrily. "You've risked all our lives to save a fucking lawyer."

"Fuck you, Dodger," she snapped back. "It wasn't you he was staring at, pleading to be let inside."

Kevin was doing his best to get the helicopter off the ground, and so far he'd managed to fly twenty feet into the air. Down below in the water, the cops in the boat had just pushed away from the dock, hollering about where to go and what to do. As

Dodger watched them, he wondered how they would fair out there. From the looks of things, they weren't working as much of a team, and if they couldn't leave the dock with any form of coordination, that bode badly for their future.

But then the first of the zombies that had been following the lawyer arrived, and that got the cops working together, and soon they were floating in the middle of the harbor and on their way. The zombies stopped at the edge of the dock, the ones in front getting shoved into the water from the ones behind pushing them. They sank like logs, only a few ripples on the surface of the water left behind after they'd sunk.

"You have any trouble getting here, Dodger?" Kevin asked as he flicked switches and the chopper rose slightly higher.

"Nah, Kevin, it was a piece of cake," he replied. He cast Pete a glance and the fat trooper only nodded, a slight grin creasing his chubby face. What had happened to the two troopers on their way to the police dock was between them, a bond of battle that had brought the two men closer. No one else needed to share in it.

"I think we're gonna be okay," Kevin said as the engine evened out and the aircraft stayed airborne. "But we're gonna be burning fuel fast, way too fast for my liking." He tapped the fuel gauge which was full at the moment. "Carrying so much weight, we're gonna need fuel before too long."

"We'll deal with it when the time comes," Dodger said. "For now just fly the damn thing."

As the helicopter rose higher into the night sky, the lighted windows of a downtown skyscraper behind the helicopter began to blink out as the power grid began to fail. A few buildings over, an explosion lit up the night and small figures could be seen falling out of the shattered windows.

Boston was dying, and it was a painful thing to watch.

As the helicopter soared off into the darkness, the five survivors knew their future was bleak, but at least with the helicopter, they had a chance to live to see the next day.

But what that day might be was something none of them was looking forward to.

Chapter 6

Dodger rubbed his eyes as the morning sun began to rise in the distance, pushing the darkness away. His eyes were heavy. He hadn't slept much since the dead began to walk, and even after they'd left Boston sleep hadn't come. He wished desperately that he could close his eyes and truly sleep for a few hours.

Behind him in the helicopter, Pam and Pete slept like logs, both of them competing for the loudest snorer award. Pete's chin still had a dusting of powdered sugar from the last snack he'd had before falling asleep. The lawyer, Goldstein was his name, they'd found out earlier, was crammed between them, his eyes wide open, his face one of total terror. The man wasn't handling the dead walking very well. His world was juries and law books, not the real world where violence seemed to be everywhere.

Dodger gazed out the plexiglass bubble to see the land below as it became more visible. They were well outside Boston now, heading west. Kevin had followed the Mass Pike, using the familiar strip of highway to take them away from the city.

They had just flown past Springfield, and the city hadn't looked too good. Fires were burning everywhere, much like Worcester had been when they'd passed it an hour ago. The Palladium and DCU center had been nothing but giant craters, thanks to a gas explosion. No more events, such as comic shows or concerts, would be held at either of the buildings ever again.

Kevin's head began to droop and Dodger leaned over and smacked Kevin in the face, making the pilot snap his head upwards.

"What the fuck!" Kevin screamed.

"You fell asleep," Dodger said.

"So you fucking hit me?" Kevin yelled.

Dodger shrugged. "It seemed like the thing to do." He pointed to the ground below them. "Why don't you find someplace to land so I can stretch my legs."

Kevin looked at the fuel gauge and nodded, while tapping it with a finger. "We need fuel anyway so sure, yeah, if I can find us someplace safe."

Dodger gazed down below where a small neighborhood was filled with men and women, all carrying guns of unknown make and model. They walked in a line while at the opposite end of the street, more people could be seen. But Dodger took one look at the second group and knew they weren't normal, that they were the living dead. "Fuck," he said as he stared at the zombies and the neighborhood watch that was just beginning to shoot them down. "This shit is all over the place. Nowhere's safe."

"You just figure that out, Einstein?" Kevin snapped, still sore from the slap in the face.

Dodger frowned but he remained silent.

"We're all gonna die," Goldstein said in a voice filled with finality. "No one's going to live through this."

"Tell me again why we took him with us?" Kevin asked, jerking his head to the back of the chopper.

Dodger shrugged again. "It seemed like the Christian thing to do at the time."

Kevin looked out at the horizon. "We're coming up on Northampton. There's a small airfield there, mostly used for Piper Cubs and a few Cessnas. Maybe we can get some more fuel there."

"Sounds like a plan. Onward, Jeeves," Dodger said with a grin.

Kevin flipped him off as he banked the aircraft slightly north, though still with a westerly heading. He was thinking if they could reach the Berkshires before running out of fuel, maybe they could find an isolated place to hole up. He knew many others that were making a run for New Hampshire and the safety of the mountains, but Kevin figured the Berkshires were just as good. Wide open country, mountainous, it was the same damn thing only no one would think to go there. The less people the better was his way of thinking.

In a few minutes, the helicopter reached the edge of the airfield. Kevin banked in wide, wanting to test the waters as it were while he approached. Once he reached the control tower, he buzzed it, going close to the windows. If there was anyone inside, they gave no sign of it.

There were a few small planes sitting just off the runway, looking like they were about to take off at any second, but the propellers were still, as was the rest of the place. Kevin flew low over the single runway, the wash from the rotor blades stirring up debris that had blown onto it. There was a small building, not much bigger than a tool shed near the end of the runway, and that was where Kevin brought the helicopter. Thirty feet from the shack was the airfield's lone two gas pumps—one for diesel and the other for unleaded.

Suddenly Pam woke up, a horrid stench filtering into her nose, then Dodger and Kevin began to make a face. Finally, Goldstein began to gag.

"Oh my God, what the fuck is that horrible stench?" Kevin asked as he fought to keep his eyes from watering.

"Jesus, I think I'm going to be sick," Goldstein said as he began to dry heave.

"I'm so sorry, guys," Pete said. He squeezed his legs as tight as they could go. "I just shit myself a little. I'm so embarrassed. I need to find a bathroom and I need to do it right now. I swear to God, if I don't I'm gonna shit my pants the rest of the way right here in this 'copter."

Gagging on the stench, Dodger said, "You heard the man, Kevin, get this bird down and fast, before we're all covered in shit." He winced. "Oh God, I think I can actually taste it, it's so bad."

"I'm going to vomit," Goldstein added, still battling his stomach to keep it down.

"But we still don't know if it's safe down there," Kevin said.

"Fuck it, Kevin," Pam snapped. "It's not safe in here!" she screamed. "Tear gas would be better than what we're being exposed to." She glared at Pete as she said this and the fat black man looked down, a hangdog look on his features.

With his free arm covering his nose and mouth, Kevin steered the helicopter towards the fuel pumps below.

Moments later, the helicopter was setting down, the rotor blades still spinning.

"I don't want to cycle down all the way," Kevin explained to Dodger. "In case we need to take off fast."

"Works for me," Dodger said as he opened the door, the sweet relief of fresh air flooding into the cockpit. Pam and Goldstein were right behind him, practically jumping out of the aircraft as soon as it touched down. Both fell to their knees where they then closed their eyes and sucked in the glorious fresh air.

Pete was also out quickly, though he began to run towards the small shack that was the airfield's office. He still had his legs squeezed together as he chanted, "One more second, just one more second. I can do it, I can do it." As he entered the office, he was already unbuckling his belt as his eyes scanned the room for a bathroom. There was a counter in the corner, what was on the other side irrelevant at the moment, a few pictures hanging on the wall of different models of personal planes, and a raggedy couch against the far wall, along with a small card table and two chairs. Then his eyes locked on a faded-white door to the right of him.

The word **Restro m** was written on it with black magic marker, one of the O's so faded it was now missing.

Pete was in it like a rocket, the single toilet beckoning to him as he dropped trou and plopped down on to the porcelain bowl. He had been in such a rush he hadn't even bothered to close the door. As loud farts and plops filled the small bathroom, he closed his eyes and leaned back, relieved and amazed that he'd managed to make it before totally ruining his underwear and pants. The small amount that was on the inside of his underwear would be easy to clean up, or he could simply remove them and go commando, but first there was only the bliss of enjoying a really good shit.

While Pete did his business, Kevin went to the fuel pumps and inspected the one that held unleaded gas, then spit and stomped his feet in disgust.

"What's wrong?" Dodger asked.

"Fucking thing's about empty. Hopefully there's enough for us to fill up, and that's only if we're really lucky."

"Every asshole in a hundred miles probably already came through here,"

Dodger said. "Doesn't matter though. As long as we get our share, that's what counts." He walked over to join Kevin.

"You got this?" Kevin asked as Dodger grabbed the gas nozzle and began dragging the hose over to the helicopter.

"Sure, I can do it. Why?"

"I figure I'll go check out that old hangar," Kevin said and did just that, wandering away to inspect an old building so dilapidated that the roof and walls looked as if they would come down in the first stiff breeze to pass by.

Dodger slid the nozzle into the slot designated for fuel. But before he did this, the trooper was going to place it in a different place, but he quickly realized it wasn't for fuel and stopped himself. He smiled, thinking what an idiot he would have been to try and put fuel in there.

Once the nozzle was securely attached, he pressed the trigger and held down on it, the fuel pumping through the hose and into the fuel tank in a steady stream. He was going to reach for a cigarette and then quickly stopped himself, once more smiling. That would be an even more stupid thing to do than where he was going to put the gas nozzle a second ago.

A noise loud enough to override the whirling rotor blades made him turn around and he was shocked to see more than a dozen zombies coming towards him. His first instinct was to reach for his sidearm, his rifle still in the cockpit, but then he saw the lead zombie climb over some crates that were just out of reach of the helicopter, and as the zombie stood up, the spinning blades took off its skull an inch above its nose. The zombie wobbled for a moment and then fell heavily to the ground, dropping to its knees as if in prayer. Meanwhile, behind it, the rest of the undead mob did the exact same thing. Soon, every skull on every zombie had been sliced off, and with arteries and veins now exposed, blood geysered up into the air, each stream a different height and size. As each zombie went to its knees and blood shot from jagged wounds, Dodger was reminded of a time he went to Las Vegas and watched a fountain in front of one of the casinos for a while—the way the blood danced in the air, much like the water spouts had done, each one going higher than the last

Without lifting a finger, the full dozen zombies were killed, and all Dodger had to do was watch the show in amazement.

Goldstein had seen the zombies, too, and his reaction had been to get back into the helicopter. The atmosphere within had aired out enough that he found it tolerable and far safer than being out in the open.

Pam had moved closer to the helicopter, but when she saw there was no danger, she'd remained standing still.

With the threat abated before it was a true threat, Dodger took out the nozzle when it clicked off and walked it back to the pump, hanging it back up. He saw that there was still a little fuel left for another hapless soul—that is, if one happened to pass by.

Kevin had reached the hangar and was searching through all the junk. As he did this, he didn't see the female zombie coming up behind him. She was wearing an office dress-suit, and from her looks, she must have come from a nearby city or town. Though there was a large chunk of her throat missing, her hair was still in remarkable good shape, and though her complexion was a pale whitish-blueish color, she was still very attractive. She actually looked quite fresh for a zombie.

She stepped on a dry twig and the crack caused Kevin to spin around to see her. Sure, he should have been freaked out that a zombie had come up on him unawares, but what he actually became was turned on. For the zombie had breasts that were huge! We're talking Dolly Parton size melons here.

Kevin stood transfixed as the zombie moved closer. She moaned once or twice and that made Kevin become even more aroused, for the moan could easily be deciphered as a sexual one.

The woman stumbled forward, and heedless of what was in her way, she didn't bother to try and move around some of the junk blocking her from Kevin. So, she ended up impaling herself on a jutting piece of rebar. The thin metal slid into her stomach, piercing her organs before popping out her back with a heavy, meaty sound reminiscent of a steak being dropped onto the floor.

She began to reach for Kevin, but was now trapped by the rebar. As she tried to struggle forward, her breasts swayed back and forth. Kevin licked his lips. She wasn't wearing a bra under her business suit. He rubbed his chin as he contemplated the scenario he now found himself in.

Hot dead chick with huge melons only a few feet away from him. No one else around at the moment.

Are you really doing anything wrong if no one is around to see it? he contemplated, mulling it over in his head, as he tried to rationalize what he wanted to do next. His growing erection, however, pretty much sealed the deal on what he was going to do.

Walking around her, he was careful to stay out of her reach. When he was behind her, he slid both hands around her waist and then moved them upwards. She snarled and moaned but couldn't grab him and a second later he had both hands on her breasts. He began to squeeze them, softly at first, then more roughly.

After less than a minute he grew bored with this and he pulled up her shirt and slid his hands across her cold flesh. His fingers found her nipples and he pinched them, all the while growing harder and more aroused.

Deciding he couldn't stand it any longer, he pulled his hands out from under her shirt and raised up her skirt. She wore panties, which were soiled in her death, and he ripped them off roughly.

Once more he looked around, wanting to make sure he was alone. He wasn't doing anything wrong, he told himself. It was no different than fucking a cow or a sheep, only this object looked like a human woman.

With her panties off, he positioned himself directly behind her, then before he could reconsider his action, he slid his member between her ass cheeks and then inside her.

His moans quickly joined hers as he began to pump for all he was worth. It wasn't warm the way a live woman's vagina would be but it was still slick and oh so tight. He closed his eyes and pumped, while the female zombie twisted and jerked on the rebar, which to Kevin felt like she was fucking him in return.

"Oh yeah, baby, fuck me," he whispered. "You're a dirty little zombie whore, aren't you? Yes you are; you're a dirty little slut." He was panting heavily as he felt himself close to orgasm. "Oh yeah, I'm gonna shoot inside you. I hope you're on the pill," he said, chuckling at his little joke. "I wouldn't want you to get pregnant or anything."

He pumped faster and faster, feeling his member getting ready to blow. His head was tilted upwards to the sky and he slammed into her harder and harder, faster and faster.

"Oh God, here it comes, baby, here it comes, here it…"

"*Kevin!* What in God's name are you *doing?*" a voice screeched from behind him, breaking his concentration. But it was too late and he shot his load deep into the zombie, then fell back and away, startled that he'd been caught fucking what was basically an animated corpse. With his pants down by his ankles, he stumbled and fell, landing hard on the ground.

"I was worried about you so I came looking for you and this is what I find?"

Kevin looked up to see Pam standing over him, her hands propped on the sides of her waist the way she was wont to do when upset. She didn't seem to care that he was naked, or that his dick was still spurting semen as it slowly deflated.

"I don't believe what I just saw," she snapped. "You were fucking that zombie!" She shook her head in amazement. "Why would you do something like that?"

Kevin's initial startlement disappeared in a flash under Pam's disproving gaze. "Because I'm fucking horny, that's why, and unlike you, *she*"—he gestured to the zombie with his chin—"didn't seem to mind a quick lay."

"But she's dead! Of course she didn't mind. You just raped a zombie," Pam screamed.

"Oh really, she's dead? Funny; she was more animated than you've ever been in the sack," he replied, while standing and pulling up his pants.

"Fuck you," she yelled. "Fuck both of you!"

"Yeah, well fuck you, too!" he yelled back. "You know, I was hoping maybe we could all get together for a threesome, but with this kind of an attitude, forget it," he said and then turned and stomped away. "And you better not tell the others about this," he called. "I know a lot of shit about you too that I can say if it comes down to it."

"Like what?" She had her arms folded across her chest.

He stopped walking and turned to face her. "Hmm, let's see. Okay, I bet the others would get a kick out of knowing how when you cum, you fart like a racehorse, or that sometimes you shit yourself if it's really intense."

Her mouth fell open in shock. "You wouldn't dare tell them. That's a secret we share as lovers."

He crossed his arms over his chest, mimicking her posture. "Try me. One word about my little fling and I'll spill it all."

She gritted her teeth for a moment in thought, her jaw growing taut, but eventually her chin loosened and she nodded slowly. "Fine, I won't say anything; you either."

Smiling, proud of himself, Kevin spun around on his heels and walked back to the helicopter, leaving Pam alone with the zombie.

"But you're still a sick fuck for what you just did," she said to his retreating back.

"That's what you love about me," he said, not bothering to turn around. "And I didn't hear her complaining. Hell, I think she might've liked it."

Pam shook her head and muttered, "How the fuck did I ever end up with such a sick bastard for a boyfriend?"

The undead woman moaned louder as Pam turned to stare at the zombie.

"Oh, you shut the fuck up, boyfriend stealer," she snapped angrily, then turned and stomped back to the helicopter.

Pete was just about finished in the office bathroom, having used an entire roll of toilet paper to clean himself up. He'd lost count at how many times he'd flushed the toilet.

He was feeling immensely better, and in fact his stomach was telling him it was ready for some more Twinkies and Ho-Hos, when he heard something moving around out in the main room, just outside the partially closed door leading to the bathroom.

"Uh hello? Anyone out there?" Pete called as he prepared to get off the toilet. "Occupado. And trust me, man, you don't want to come in here after me."

The noise continued unabated, but for the life of him he couldn't figure out what it was.

Feeling vulnerable on the can, and figuring he should pull his pants up and prepare for the worst, he stood up, but before he could reach down and grab the waistband of his pants, two small children—a boy and a girl—no more than ten, came charging into the bathroom. By their complexions it was clear to Pete they were both zombies.

Before Pete could do anything, the two undead tykes were on him, their mouths trying to bite him. But being that they were only even with his waist, the closest thing to try and bite was Pete's dick. Though he couldn't actually see his penis, due to his bulk, Pete felt the cold breath of the two kids as they tried to rip his dick off his body.

"Jesus-fucking-Christ!" Pete screamed as he fell back against the dirty sink, his arm hitting the already-cracked mirror and sending a dozen reflective-shards falling to the white-tiled floor. "Get the hell away from me!"

In response, the kids renewed their attack, wanting that dick for all they were worth. Pete shoved the girl away from him, the small form flying across the bathroom and out the door. Now he only had to contend with the boy, who was as ferocious as a wild animal.

Teeth clacking, the boy was doing his best to get at Pete's dick, but no matter how hard he tried, Pete managed to get away. If someone had been watching, from a first glance, it would have seemed that Pete was a pedophile, trying to get with the boy, but if anyone had cared to watch longer, then things would have seemed vastly different from that first impression. For one thing, the back of the boy's neck had a terrible wound on it, blood having soaked into his shirt and across his back.

The girl had a bloody wound on her arm and one cheek was missing, the bite marks terrible. It was evident the boy had become a zombie and had then attacked the sister, both becoming zombies. Now they were in the mood for some dark meat, and Pete was on the menu.

Pete tried to grab the revolver on his belt but it was tangled up in his pants. He should have taken it out before sitting on the toilet but he'd been in far too much of a rush to think of such things. Now it was going to be the death of him. *Well*, he thought, *at least I got one last good shit in before I die.*

Tripping over his pants, he fell to the floor, the boy right with him. The undead kid was about to get himself an all beef hotdog, and Pete knew he needed to act fast or he was about to become a eunuch. He'd never had much luck with the ladies, and without a dick there would never even be so much as a hint of hope, plus jerking off would become a hell of a lot more difficult without a dick.

As if Pete didn't have enough to deal with, the girl was back, having gotten up. One of her arms was broken now, the one without the wound, but she didn't seem to mind too much. She got on her knees and began to crawl towards Pete's wide-open legs, his dangling balls and dick looking like low-hanging fruit. Pete kicked the boy in the face and then the girl, one with each foot. As they flew backwards to bounce off the doorframe, Pete struggled to get his pants back on, though now that he was flat on his back it was all the more difficult. A few pieces of the broken mirror cut his ass and he winced. The cuts weren't serious but they still hurt.

Struggling with his pants, he could hear the two undead cherubs getting back to their feet, but knowing what was coming, Pete redoubled his efforts, and in seconds flat managed to get his pants up. He only slipped them up, not having time to zip up or button them, as the kids were back at the doorway, ready to attack once more.

"You little fucks," Pete hissed, his usual pleasant demeanor now gone. Bending over, he picked up a piece of mirrored-glass in both hands. The glass cut his palms slightly but his thick calluses from working construction before joining the police force served him well now. He was angry, far angrier than he should have been. He knew emotion wasn't something that should be entertained when dealing with zombies, but these little fucks had tried to bite his dick off. He wasn't about to forgive and forget that incident in a hurry.

The two children came at him again, snarling and growling like little animals, but Pete was ready for them this time, and as they moved forward, he stabbed the glass into both their eyes, the left eye for the boy, who was on his right, and the girl's right eye, as she was to his left. The sharp shards slid into the eyes easily, slicing into the orbs as if they were hard-boiled eggs. A pinkish-whitish ooze squirted out around the shards as the tips were forced deep into the small craniums. As the two little zombies stopped their attack, Pete then kicked each one in the chest, sending them back out the bathroom doorway—this the last time.

The two bodies fell to the floor in small heaps, Pete right behind them. One at a time, he stomped on their faces, crushing their skulls into a bloody pulp. When he was finished and came out of his fugue state of anger, he was winded, and his right boot was covered in gore.

Turning to leave, knowing he should get back to the others, and not wanting to be left behind, he found that there was an adult zombie standing in the doorway to the office. Pete reached down for his sidearm, planning on blowing the zombie away, when suddenly shots rang out from outside, and a bullet zipped past the zombie's head and took off a piece of Pete's ear.

"Jesus Christ!" he screamed, dropping to the floor as the zombie, heedless of the bullets being fired at it, shuffled into the office, its eyes locked on Pete's prone form.

More bullets zipped through the air and another caught Pete in the upper left arm. It was a glancing blow, a flesh wound, but it still stung like a bastard. Pete crawled behind a desk to seek more cover. "Stop firing! Someone's in here!" he screamed but it didn't stop the shooter. The bullets screamed through the air, the far wall becoming pockmarked with bullet holes. There was a bulletin board there, notes littering it from end to end. The words had been written haphazardly, the people in a rush, and as Pete cowered behind the desk he scanned them briefly.

"Tom, with everything that's happened, I've decided to leave you for your brother. Goodbye forever. BTW: You were terrible in bed— Sarah."

Another read: "Dick, you suck, I wish I never met you. Don't try to find me, I've gone to another city and changed my name— formerly Sue."

Yet another read: "Mike, I've embezzled all the funds from the company and am making a run for another country. See ya later, sucker—Bill."

"Shit," Pete mumbled, "the people around here are a bunch of assholes."

Pete poked his head from around the desk to see out the doorway leading outside, where he saw Goldstein with a high-powered rifle, taking shots at Pete's location. The lawyer couldn't shoot for shit, which explained why Pete had been shot not once but twice.

"Hey, you asshole, stop shooting at me!" Pete yelled, but his voice was lost in the reports of more gunshots. Pete had to duck back behind the desk or risk being hit. Shuffling feet caused Pete to look over his shoulder to see the zombie that had come into the office standing there. It was already bending over to grab Pete's foot, when suddenly its head exploded, raining blood and bone matter, along with a healthy amount of pus-coated brains, onto Pete, who covered his head and buried his face into the floor.

The body fell over to the left and landed in a heap of flesh, now nothing but a lump of rotting meat.

"Hey, Pete, you in there? You all right?" Dodger called from outside.

Pete peered from around the desk to see Dodger standing next to Goldstein, only now Dodger was holding the rifle. He'd taken it from the lawyer and swiftly and skillfully put down the zombie.

"Yeah, I'll live," Pete called back as he got to his feet. "Barely!" He used the desk to heave his bulk up. His arm and ear were bleeding still but the wounds were already slowing. He'd been lucky and knew it. But none of it would have happened if not for Goldstein.

After making sure his pants were secured and the belt tightened, Pete stomped outside, marching directly for Goldstein, who was standing stock still, looking lost. When Dodger saw that Pete was fine and exiting the building, he turned and went back to the helicopter, wanting to keep an eye on it. Now that it was fueled they would all be leaving shortly.

"I'm glad to see you're okay," Goldstein said as Pete stomped towards him. "I saw that zombie and grabbed a rifle from the helicopter, but I'm not very good with it, as you just found out."

Pete said nothing as he pulled his sidearm and aimed it right at Goldstein, whose face lit up with terror.

"What are you…" was all the lawyer managed to say before Pete punched him in the face, sending Goldstein to the ground with a bloody nose. But before Goldstein could cry out, Pete leveled the gun in his hand at Goldstein's lower leg and fired, sending a bullet into the lawyer's leg.

Goldstein screamed as the bullet tore into his flesh and then lodged into the dirt beneath him. Pete, though angry, had still fired so that the bullet barely grazed the man.

"Jesus Christ, you fucking shot me! What the hell was that for?" Goldstein screamed as he grabbed his leg, small spurts of blood shooting around his fingers. His gray slacks immediately became soaked in blood.

"I shot you 'cause you shot me twice, you goddamn honkey! Shit, I'm lucky you didn't kill me! What the fuck were you thinking, just shooting into that building like that?" He grinned. "Hurts don't it? How do you like it, motherfucker?"

Dodger walked over and stopped when he was ten feet away. He took in the situation immediately and said, "Pete, you gonna kill him or what? We need to go. Kevin is firing up the bird and Pam's already inside."

Pete glanced at Dodger, the gun still aimed at Goldstein. "And what If I did want to kill this cracker? Would you stop me?"

Dodger shrugged. "There's been so much death lately, one more won't matter too much. Just shoot the fucker in the head so he don't come back." Dodger turned and walked away, the matter over for him. He probably should have tried to stop Pete, but he was fairly confident Pete wouldn't shoot the man, or so he hoped.

Goldstein's eyes went wide upon realizing Pete had a free hand to kill him. "No, wait, I'm sorry, I'm so fucking sorry. I shouldn't have tried to kill that zombie. I know that now. I was stupid, cocky. Please don't kill me, Pete, I'm begging you. I don't want to d…d…die," he stammered out, crying heavily as tears rolled down his face and he wet his pants.

Pete started at the prone man and shook his head in disgust, then lowered the gun. "Shit man, I wasn't gonna kill ya, just scare ya a little. Christ, pull yourself together, man." He turned and walked back to the helicopter. "Goddamn honkey cracker; too fucking stupid to hold a gun. I shoulda capped his white skinny ass anyway." He was halfway from Goldstein when he yelled, "Come on, white boy, get up and follow me or I'll make Kevin leave you behind!"

Goldstein, sniffing loudly, managed to get up, and begin hobbling back to the helicopter, wincing each time he took a step.

Kevin had gone through his preflight and was ready to takeoff when first Pete, then Goldstein arrived and got in. Kevin saw the lawyer's leg but said nothing, not wanting to get in the middle of whatever had happened. Pam, seeing the man's leg, ripped some of her shirt off and used it as a bandage. As soon as she applied pressure, the wound slowed to a stop. Pete saw this out of the corner of his eye and nodded to himself. His shot had been well-aimed, and hadn't struck anything major. The man would live, maybe have a limp, but he wouldn't shoot at people without thinking ever again.

"You didn't kill him, huh?" Dodger asked Pete, upon seeing the lawyer's bleeding leg.

Pete shrugged. "Didn't seem to be a need. He learned his lesson."

"I figured that, too," Dodger nodded, the matter settled. "I figured you weren't a murderer, Pete."

Kevin began working the controls and the helicopter began to rise. More zombies could be seen approaching the fuel pumps now that the chopper was high in the air. There had to be more than a hundred, coming in from all sides. Dodger frowned. If they hadn't left when they did, they would have quickly found themselves inundated.

"Shit, look at all of them down there," Dodger said as the helicopter banked west and began flying away.

"They sure are everywhere," Pete added.

"I'm going to sue your ass off," Goldstein mumbled. "You just wait."

Pete turned to look at the man. "You say something, white boy? I heard you muttering something but I'll be damned if I know what it was."

Goldstein swallowed the knot in his throat. "I...I said I'm gonna sue your ass for attempted murder the first chance I get. You'll pay for shooting me. When I shot you it was an accident, I was trying to save you, but this was intentional." He gestured with his chin at his leg.

Dodger, sitting in the front seat besides Kevin, shifted so that he was looking behind him at Goldstein. "You really don't get it, do you, pal. There's probably not gonna be a world where shit like suing people is going to be around. Things have changed, and not for the better."

"That's ridiculous," the lawyer replied. "You're a fool for even thinking such a thing. You're all fools. You should listen to me. I'm smart. I'm a fucking lawyer. For Christ's sake, I went to Yale. I know what I'm talking about. This isn't permanent. The dead will be taken care of. The military will…"

"The military isn't gonna do shit," Dodger spat. "Don't you get it? Every time someone dies they get back up and become one of them. There's no stopping this, at least, not by using violence."

"So what's the alternative?" Pam asked, curious to the answer.

Dodger shrugged. "I have no fucking idea. But I'm for heading for the hills, finding a place to put my feet up, stock up with a few cases of beer and food, and then I'm gonna relax and let the shit take care of itself."

"Fools, all of you." Goldstein said, as he crossed his arms over his chest and pouted. He glared at Pete, who sat beside him, wishing he could deal with the man now. But Pete was almost twice the size of the lawyer, and though a lot of it was body fat, it still made a physical confrontation out of the question. Goldstein would have to bide his time and wait for his chance to get even. He felt braver now that he was with the others.

"Hey, look over there," Kevin said, pointing out past the windshield at a spec on the horizon.

"It's another chopper," Dodger said.

"Who do you think it is?" Pam asked.

Dodger gave her one of his patented shrugs. "No idea, but if it's military or police, we don't want them catching us."

"Why not?" Goldstein asked.

Kevin was the one to respond. "Because I didn't exactly get permission to take this bird, that's why."

"You mean you stole it?" Goldstein asked, his face one of shock. "You mean I'm an accomplice to a felony?"

Dodger made a clicking sound out of the corner of his mouth. "I didn't see you minding any when there were two dozen zombies on your ass back at the dock. And even if I'd clarified matters back then, would it have mattered to you?"

"Well, I don't know. I mean, I'm a lawyer after all. I'm an officer of the court. I can't take part in a crime, and a felony no less!"

"That chopper's getting closer," Kevin said. "What should I do?"

"Try and lose him," Dodger said.

"How do I do that?" Kevin asked, turning his head so he was looking directly at Dodger. "I'm a news anchor and new to flying as well. I sure as shit don't have experience in dogfights."

Dodger frowned. "Just turn away from the other chopper and fly faster than it. Shit, Kevin, I don't know. Try and see if we can lose it long enough for you to set this thing down where we won't be seen."

Kevin banked the helicopter north, putting his tail to the other aircraft, then throttled higher so that the helicopter began to lean slightly forward as it picked up speed. The motor grew louder as Kevin pushed the engine as fast as he could. "You know, this is going to burn a lot of our fuel!" he told Dodger and the others. He had to yell to be heard over the thrumming engine.

"One thing at a time, Kevin. We need to shake them before our fuel situation even matters," Dodger said.

"My God!" Pam yelled to he heard. "This is all so crazy. We have no idea where we're going and now we're being chased by God knows who. Kevin, maybe we should go back to the city. If you return the helicopter maybe no one will press charges. Just look at you, you're exhausted. You need to rest, sleep for a bit."

"I for one agree with Pam," Goldstein added. "We should go back to Boston."

"Shut the fuck up," Pete snapped at Goldstein. "No one cares what you think."

Goldstein glared at Pete but he said nothing in response.

"We're not going back," Kevin said while he shook his head, and glanced over his shoulder to make eye contact with Pam. They had just had a fight, sure, but despite that he still loved her. He knew once they were finally alone they would talk it out, and then maybe even have makeup sex if there was time. Their relationship had always been rocky, when he thought about it. They would argue over the silliest things, then later would make up, having fantastic sex, and then once more all would be good between them. It was a strange dynamic, but it was one that worked well for them. Pam was a spitfire; it was one of the things that had attracted her to him when they'd first met. But sometimes her willfulness, her stubbornness, could be frustrating, maddening even. But then he would think about her naked body; her small but perky breasts, her flat stomach, her tight little ass, and the little mustache she shaved over her pussy, and anything and everything simply fell away as irrelevant. He guessed he was pussy-whipped, but as he thought about how tight she was and the way she would ride him like a cowboy riding a bucking bull, well, being whipped didn't seem like such a bad thing.

Dodger pointed to a string of buildings off to the left, more than a quarter mile away. "There, Kevin, go over there. Maybe there's a parking garage or something where you can set down."

Pam looked out the side window behind the helicopter and said, "Whoever's following us is a little closer. I can see that it's painted green."

"Shit, that's definitely military," Dodger said. "Army or National Guard maybe.

"Does it matter which one?" Pete asked, adding his voice to the mix.

"No, not really. One's the same as the other given the circumstances," Dodger replied.

"What do we do if they catch us?" Pete asked.

Dodger shrugged, the gesture involuntary. "That's something I don't want to find out. Let's hope Kevin here is as good a pilot as he thinks he is."

"Fuck you," Kevin snapped back, though it was with a grin. "Hold on, folks, I'm gonna push the engine to the max. I don't know about you, but I don't feel like getting arrested today."

The helicopter surged forward, the needle on the dashboard sliding into the red as Kevin pushed the motor for all it was worth. The sudden rush sent everyone's heads but Kevin's against the backrests from the sudden jolt. Kevin's jaw was set fast, his eyes locked on the slowly growing string of buildings before him. This was his helicopter now, and he'd be damned if he was going to let someone take it away from him.

Chapter 7

"Will you please move over, there's hardly any room for me to breathe,"

Pam snapped.

"I'm over as far as I can go," Pete snapped back.

"Then make your ass smaller because I can't keep getting squished like this."

"My ass is fine for my body, and you should talk," Pete quipped.

Pam's mouth fell open in shock. "Are you seriously comparing my ass to yours? Because believe me, you'll lose that bet."

"If you two don't behave, I swear I'll turn this helicopter around and we can go back to Boston," Kevin said with a light-hearted tone, as if the two squabbling adults were his children. "Now you two better behave or else."

"I want to go back to Boston," Goldstein said, not getting the joke at all. "Let's go back right now." Goldstein had become even more of an irritant since the helicopter had left the small airfield. He constantly complained and whined about where they were going, how his leg hurt, how none of them had an idea of what they were doing.

Pete leaned in close to Pam and said under his breath, "I swear, if this guy doesn't shut the hell up, I'm gonna throw him out of this chopper."

Pam snorted. "You wouldn't dare. You're a cop after all, you're supposed to serve and protect."

"Oh yeah? Well, honey, maybe it's time I served and protected 'myself' for a change. It might not have been a long time since I met Dodger, but I've realized a lot of things since then; namely that I need to suck it up and pull my weight better."

Pam looked at him with bored eyes. "Well, that's a hell of a lot of weight to pull, if you ask me." She might have taken Pete seriously if the fat man hadn't been shoving his mouth full of Ho-Ho's and Twinkies while he talked. Crumbs fell down his shirt and covered the front of his uniform, making him look like a messy child; he had a bad habit of talking with his mouth full, too. Pam tried to look the other way, any way other than at that portal of a mouth, with its mushed-up pastry within.

"Hey, there's something up ahead," Dodger said, sitting up in his seat so he could see the horizon better.

"I don't know this area," Kevin added. "Never been up here much."

"Me neither," Dodger said, then turned to look at the others. "Any of you?"

Pam and Goldstein shook their heads, Pete shrugging.

The cockpit was silent for the next minute and a half as the helicopter flew closer to what Dodger had spotted.

Finally, Dodger said, "Oh shit, it's a shopping mall. A big one by the looks of it." There was a giant sign in the parking lot. **CRYSTAL MALL** was written in large, bold letters on the white facade. At night the sign would be lit up, so that all arriving could see the glorious monument to consumerism.

"Hey, we could go there," Kevin suggested as he approached the sprawling building. "I could land on the roof, too." He frowned as he studied the fuel gauge. "We're low on gas too, so better that we pick the spot than have us run out and have to drop down somewhere we have no control of."

"Yeah, but would it be safe there?" Pam asked.

"Sure," Dodger replied. "And if there aren't too many other survivors there, it would be a real good place to hole up for a while."

"You can't go there," Goldstein said, his voice one of authority.

"Why the fuck not?" Pete asked, now that he'd swallowed his food. He stared at Goldstein angrily, a perpetual dislike for the man having crept into his heart. You couldn't really blame Pete for it; after all, the lawyer had shot him—twice.

"Because you don't want to get sued," Goldstein replied, his face set in a tone that would brook no argument.

"What the hell are you talking about?" Dodger asked.

"A shopping mall, zombies—it's not somewhere you all can go. If you do, I warn you, you're gonna be in a lot of trouble."

"That's the most ridiculous thing I ever heard," Kevin said. "You can't own something like zombies in a shopping mall. To even think such a thing is ridiculous. You can't copyright one particular situation."

"Whether it's ridiculous or not is irrelevant. All that matters is that a hurt party can sue—even if they're totally full of shit. It doesn't matter if they're just money-grubbing, and trying to take advantage of a situation. If they think they can make a buck on it, there are people that feel they own everything. This is one such instance." He crossed his arms over his chest as if he was holding his heart in. "I won't be a part of it. I want you to let me out of here this instant."

Dodger looked at Kevin and said, "The guy's gone nuts. He's fucking babbling. Do you get what he's talking about?"

"Don't look at me. I see nothing wrong with us going to the mall. As long as what we do there are our own actions, and not someone else's. That we do things the way 'we' want to do them, I think it's what they call 'fair use.' "

Dodger blinked. "I have no idea what you just said. Is everyone going crazy around here?"

"No, I won't go there, you can't make me," Goldstein was yelling as Pete tried to calm him down. "No, let me out of here. I'll scream, so help me. You're all gonna be sorry if you go there, mark my words!" It was getting pretty serious as Goldstein began to punch and kick, heedless of his bullet wound. Kevin got whacked on the head twice and the helicopter began to rock as his grip on the controls faltered.

"Ow!" Pam yelled when she got an elbow to the face from Goldstein, who was becoming increasingly violent. The situation was getting worse by the second and Dodger was reaching down to pull his sidearm, deciding if Goldstein didn't stop it, the trooper was going to have to shoot him, when the cockpit door was thrown open and suddenly Goldstein was flying out of the chopper, and falling to earth like a rock.

"You'll be sorry!" he screamed as he plummeted to the ground below. But he didn't die when his body impacted the ground, for there was a half-filled pool below him in a backyard of a two-family home. Goldstein hit the water like a brick, but he survived, and a second later was bobbing on the surface. Kevin had swung the helicopter around to see where Goldstein had landed and the lawyer was waving a fist upwards. "You'll all be sorry! Mark my words! Don't go to that shopping mall; go somewhere else!"

"Jesus, what a nutjob," Kevin said and swung the chopper around and back to its original heading.

Dodger glanced over his shoulder at Pete, who had been the one to throw Goldstein out of the helicopter. "You know, I was about to shoot the fucker if you hadn't done that, Pete. Good work."

Pete shrugged. "It had to be done. The guy was nuts."

"Well, Pete, it was nice of you to throw him out when there was a pool below. He never would have survived that fall if not," Dodger said.

Pete shrugged again, then opened a box of Twinkies and ate half of one with a single bite. "I guess so. Truth be told, I didn't know there was a pool down there."

"You mean..." Dodger began.

"You got it; white boy got lucky," Pete said around a mouthful of yellow and creme mush.

As the helicopter approached the shopping mall, Dodger began to laugh, and soon the others were joining in. Finally, even Pete began to chuckle once he got the joke.

As the last of the laughter died down—which had taken a while due to everyone using it as an excuse to release the stress they all felt—the news helicopter settled onto the roof of the shopping mall at the north corner.

"Are you sure the roof will hold us?" Pam asked as Kevin began cycling down the engine, the rotors already slowing so that they could be seen individually as they spun around overhead.

"We'll find out the hard way if it doesn't," Kevin replied. When he was finished turning off the engine, he opened his door and climbed out, Dodger doing the same on the opposite side. Pam and Pete were right behind them.

There were raised sunroofs made of plexiglass scattered across the roof, these here so that the mall would have natural light during the day. Kevin and Dodger went to one of them, then peered down into the shopping mall.

Zombies could be seen moving around the mall, some seeming to be doing things that they did in life. One zombie exited a store selling kitchen accessories, a microwave cord wrapped around its leg. As the zombie shuffled, the microwave was dragged behind it. The door to the appliance was open, and it flapped around like a dead bird's beak. Many more wandered around aimlessly, resembling the senior citizens who would walk the mall every morning for exercise.

Looking at the far end of the hallway below, a water fountain could be seen. The water was on and the stream was lit up with greens and reds, oscillating back and forth. At the other end of the hallway, were three more hallways joined together in a main junction, an escalator could be seen. A few zombies were on it, riding up one side, then they would go to the 'down' side and ride that back to the main floor. Around and around they went.

"Looks like the power's still on here," Dodger said. "That's a good thing."

As if the entire shopping mall heard him speak, the fountains suddenly stopped flowing, the escalators stopped moving, and the entire mall went dark, with the exception of where natural light flooded in through the skylights. "Oops, I spoke too soon," he said.

"You jinxed us," Pam said. "Nice going."

"I doubt Dodger saying it made it happen," Kevin said to Pam. "Besides, the power actually being on seemed pretty much impossible. I mean, if this was a movie, I guess the power would have to be on, otherwise there would be a complication for the characters, but still, it would be one hell of a plot hole to anyone who wanted to really pay attention."

"Well, it's too bad we're not in a movie then," Dodger said. "Because electricity would have been really nice to have." He tapped on the glass, causing a few zombies to look up at him and the others. One zombie raised its hand and flipped off Dodger, who promptly blinked in surprise. "Did that zombie down there just give me the finger?"

"Which one?"' Pam asked.

Dodger pointed. "That one."

Pam squinted as she studied the zombie, then shook her head. "You're mistaken. It looks like his fingers are broken. It just 'looks' like he did."

"Oh, good. I can handle the dead walking, but if the dead are assholes too, well, that's a whole other ballgame."

"Let's see if there's a way inside," Kevin said, stepping away from the skylight, Pam and Pete joining him.

The second they left—leaving only Dodger peering down into the mall—the same zombie that had flipped him off turned around, bent over, and pulled down its pants, after which it began waving its pale ass back and forth.

"What the fuck? Hey, guys, that zombie is mooning me."

"What?" Pete asked, turning to look at Dodger as he walked away.

"That zombie down there. The one that gave me the finger. Now it's gone and mooned me."

"What? Let me see, that's ridiculous." Pete walked back until he was by Dodger's side again. Gazing down into the mall, the same zombie was there, but now its pants were up and it was simply looking up at the skylight, while a few others around it did the same thing.

"I don't see anything out of the ordinary down there," Pete said. "Just zombies doing their thing."

"But I saw. I mean, I swear that it…"

Pete placed a hand on Dodger's shoulder. "It's okay, buddy, we're all a little tired. You must have imagined it." He walked away to join Pam and Kevin, leaving Dodger standing with his mouth hanging open.

"But I swear I saw…" He gazed down into the mall, his focus jumping from one zombie to the next. They all looked the same now: pale faces, dried blood here and there on their clothes, greasy hair. Now he couldn't even figure out which one had mooned him. Shaking his head as if to clear it, he said under his breath, "I must be losing it." Then he pushed off the skylight and ran after the others while below, the zombies milled about.

Halfway across the rooftop, Kevin and Pete, with Pam behind them, stopped by another skylight. They were still peering down into the mall when Dodger caught up to them.

"What's so interesting?" Dodger asked upon joining the others.

Kevin gestured down through the skylight. "The mall isn't down there. It's something else. It's dark, too."

Dodger joined Kevin and gazed down through the glass. "Maybe it's a storeroom of some kind. That would be good. Maybe it's separate from the mall and there aren't any zombies down there."

"But how do we get down there?" Pete asked.

Dodger looked around the roof, and upon spotting a ladder left there by some past maintenance worker, he grinned and said, "Like this," and promptly used the butt of his rifle to shatter one of the panels. As plexiglass rained down to the darkness below, he retrieved the ladder. He had a smug look on his face, like he was macho or something, for breaking the panel.

Pete was frowning.

"What?" Dodger asked.

"Shit, man, I could have done that. Any of us could have done that," Pete said.

"I could have done that easy," Pam added.

"Sure, me too," Kevin said. "Hell, even Goldstein could have done it."

"What are you guys getting at?" Dodger asked.

Pete shrugged. "Nothing. It's just, don't go and act all cool 'cause you broke a window. It's not that big of a deal."

"Whatever," Dodger replied and slid the ladder into the darkness through the skylight opening. Then he climbed down, jumping off the last of the rungs to land lightly on his feet. "Assholes," he muttered under his breath. "It was cool. They were all like: 'Oh no, how are we gonna get in there?' And I was like, smash, 'Here's how, bitches.' "

"What do you see?" Kevin called down from above.

Dodger looked up to see Kevin's head, along with the others, silhouetted by the sky. "Right now, all I see is shit," he called up.

"Should we come down?" Kevin called.

"In a second; just let me make sure it's clear down here," Dodger replied and moved off deeper into the darkness. He pulled a small penlight from a pocket and turned it on. The small beam pierced the blackness easily.

Suddenly, two zombies came out of the darkness, both covered in blood and gore. How they had ended up in this part of the mall was unknown— not that it mattered. What did was that both zombies were hungry for flesh, namely Dodger's.

The surprised trooper was totally caught off guard, and he was knocked to the floor, his rifle sliding away to hit the far wall. The zombies fell on him in an instant, their teeth snapping at his throat, his nose, his cheeks, anywhere there was exposed flesh. Punching and shoving, Dodger did his best to fend them off, but he was outnumbered and on his back on the floor. He was far too vulnerable for his liking, and if he didn't act fast, he was going to end up dead.

Pushing the zombie on his right away from him, he took that second of respite and reached down to his side for his Bowie knife. For a brief second he couldn't find it and began to panic, but then his hand rested on the hilt, and he pulled it from its sheath and brought it up before him.

When the zombie came back after being forced away, Dodger had the knife before him, and he thrust it into the zombie's right eye, the tip sliding through the orb and deep into the brain. The zombie went slack almost immediately, but as it fell to the floor, it took the knife with it, twisting Dodger's wrist. He cried out as he let go of the knife and then yelled out again when the other zombie sank its teeth into his left arm, just above his wrist.

"Shit," he yelled as teeth clamped down on bone. Using his free hand, he reached out for the knife again, and after grabbing it by the hilt, he yanked it free of the very-dead zombie's head. Bringing it up and around in an arc, the now-bloodied tip slid into the ear of the attacking zombie, slicing through the ear canal and into the brain. The zombie bucked once and went limp, falling on top of Dodger, who found himself trapped under the 'dead' weight of the corpse.

"Dodger, are you all right?" a voice called down from the skylight.

He didn't know who the owner was and it didn't really matter. "I'm fine, give me a second."

"What's going on down there?" It was Pete's voice. "Do you need my help?"

"No, Pete, I'm fine. I said to give me a goddamn second." Shifting his hips, Dodger managed to slide out from under the zombie. Angry at what it had done to him, he quickly bandaged his arm with a piece of material torn from the bottom of his shirt. Then, still upset, he began hacking at the zombie's neck, not stopping until the head was severed from the body.

"Dodger, you okay?" Kevin called down nervously.

"Maybe I should go down there," Pete said, looking at the others for their agreement.

"But Dodger said to wait here," Pam replied.

"Dodger's not the boss of me," Pete scoffed. "I can go where I like."

Suddenly, a roundish object came spinning up through the broken skylight, while from below, Dodger called out, "Heads up, guys!"

At first, none of the three understood what was happening, but then the object landed on the rooftop between them and Pam looked down first.

"Fuck me!" she screamed. "Get it away from me—gross!"

The severed head was still gnashing its mouth, as it tried to take a bite out of Pam's shoe. Reacting quickly, she swung her foot back and then kicked the head like it was a ball, sending it bouncing and rolling across the rooftop. It didn't stop until it connected with an air conditioning unit, the sound of the head striking the aluminum reverberating across the roof in a dull thud. Lying on its right cheek, the head still twitched, the mouth opening and closing, the tongue sliding across cracked lips, the eyes flicking back and forth.

Dodger's head appeared in the broken skylight as he popped up, a slim smile on his lips.

"You asshole," Pam snapped. "That wasn't funny."

"Yeah it was," Dodger replied. "Well, a little anyways."

Pam slapped Kevin on the arm. "Are you going to let him get away with that? Do something? He's your friend, damn it."

Kevin shrugged. "What do you want me to do about it, Pam? Beat Dodger up?" He smiled slightly. "It was 'kinda' funny."

"Yeah, Pam," Pete added. "You should've seen your face."

"Fuck you, Pete, and you too, Kevin. You know what? Fuck all of you. Men," she growled and stomped across the roof to the edge overlooking the parking lot.

"Pam, wait a sec..." Kevin began but Dodger cut him off.

"Let her go," Dodger said. "She'll cool off in a bit. Besides, there's more important shit to deal with. You two need to come down here and see what I found."

"Anything good?" Kevin asked.

"Just follow me. It's easier to show than tell you." Dodger's face disappeared back into the skylight as he climbed down the ladder. Kevin went next and then Pete, who had a little trouble getting his wide girth through the skylight. Like Pooh in a tree looking for a honey pot, he honestly thought he was going to get stuck, then at the last instant he popped free and was sliding down the ladder.

Pam watched Pete disappear into the skylight, then she turned and faced the parking lot below. Zombies were everywhere, stumbling around and bumping into things. She was angry at Dodger for his practical joke, but there was something else bothering her.

She was pregnant, and though she'd been with Kevin for more than six months, she'd had an affair with one of the anchorman at the television station. She'd ended it more than three weeks ago, but not before finding out that she was two months or so pregnant, after going in to get a checkup when she was late on her period. She'd never been late before, it came like clockwork, so after a full month and it still hadn't come, she'd gone in to see her doctor. The news was what she expected, though she wasn't pleased with it.

She hadn't had the heart to tell Kevin yet, and if being pregnant wasn't bad enough, then the fact that the child wasn't Kevin's would only add to the difficult situation.

That was enough to make any woman worry, but now she found herself in a world where the dead walked and society was crumbing. What was she supposed to do now? What would she do in six or so months when the child was due to be born? Would things be better by then? Or would it be even worse than it was now? All these questions swirled in her head, making her dizzy just thinking about it. As a matter of fact, she took a few steps away from the edge of the roof, not wanting to fall over.

She waited for another five minutes, until she felt she'd calmed down enough to join the men. She wondered if it was hormones that had made her get so upset over Dodger's joke. She knew by overreacting she only added to his amusement, and that if she'd simply shrugged it off as an annoyance, the matter would have been dropped almost immediately. But instead she'd blown up, cursing and yelling, before storming off across the roof to brood.

Yes, it must be hormones.

Deciding she would try and keep herself under better control, she went to the skylight and climbed down through the broken window, landing softly at the bottom after the swift descent. The men were in the next room, and other than Dodger and Pete's flashlight beams bouncing off the walls from the next room, and what wan light filtered in through the skylight, the room was pretty much wreathed in darkness.

Stepping away from the ladder, she almost tripped over the two zombies prone on the floor—one minus a head. She was about to cry out in disgust but she clamped a hand over her mouth to stop herself. What had she just deiced on the roof? Moving around the corpses, she fast-walked across the room until she was in the next one, joining the three men, who were talking.

Dodger was holding a small jar in his right hand, while his left patted an open box, one of dozens stacked up against the wall.

"There's enough of this stuff to keep us fat and happy for a year, maybe longer."

"Yeah, but baby food?" Kevin said. "I have a four-year-old niece. One time I fed her when she was a baby, and I tried some of the strained peas out of curiosity. It tasted like bland mush."

"Well, yeah, the taste isn't that great, but there's plenty of nutrients, vitamins and the like to keep us fed. That's what matters here," Dodger said.

Pete picked up a jar out of the open box, cracked the lid, and sniffed the contents. It was strained carrots. His nose wrinkled but he shrugged and said, "Well then, there's no time like the present. I'm starving." He drank the carrots, shaking the jar to get the orange mush out. The jar wasn't large, about two inches tall and the same around. Pete had downed all of it in two gulps. Wiping his mouth with the back of his sleeve, he added, "Not bad. If you take it down like a shot of alcohol, you barely taste it."

Pam pushed past Kevin, picking up a jar and inspecting it, then studying the other boxes. A few boxes had a picture of a water drop on them, while the rest were all baby food. "Shit, it sure seems convenient that all this stuff is here, right when we need it the most. It's like it was waiting here just for us, and in a shopping mall of all places. If this was a movie, this would be yet another giant plot hole."

Dodger snatched the jar from her hand, an angry look on his face. "Then it's a good thing this isn't a movie. You don't have to eat it if you don't want to."

She snatched it back. "I didn't say I wouldn't eat it, just that it's awfully convenient. I'm starving and food is food."

"Damn straight," Dodger said and tossed more jars to the others.

"What about spoons?" Kevin asked, catching a jar of strained peas in his right hand.

"Don't have any. Just drink it," Dodger said and did just that. He tipped a jar of mushed carrots over his upturned mouth and chugged it down easily, like Pete had done. The jars were small, so that it would take two dozen to satiate his hunger and probably double that to fill Pete.

After eating three jars, Dodger wiped his mouth on the back of his sleeve. "Shit, this is gonna get old real fast. Hell, I'd be happy with some SPAM right about now."

"You and me both, man," Pete said, Kevin agreeing. Pam said nothing, but silently nursed her jar of mushed green beans. The baby on the side of the jar kept staring at her, or so it seemed. It was probably because she knew she was pregnant. She knew when that happened, it was like everything and anything would remind a mother-to-be about babies.

Kevin saw Pam staring at the jar and he joined her. "What's wrong with you? You have that look again. The last time was a week ago, before the dead began walking. We were watching TV and a commercial came on about diapers. I saw you start to tear up. You didn't think I noticed but I did."

"I'm fine, Kevin, just leave me alone."

"No, Pam, I won't," he said, then grabbed her by the arm and dragged her away from the others so they could get some privacy.

"Uh-oh, looks like there's trouble in Love Town," Pete joked as he cracked open another jar and began gulping it down. Already his shirt was covered with bits of mush of various colors.

"Take it easy on that stuff, Pete," Dodger said. "Or you're gonna be shittin' out your insides in a bit."

"Ah, I'll be fine," Pete said as he finished off the jar, licking his finger after scraping the inside of it.

"You're what?" Kevin suddenly yelled from across the room, causing Dodger and Pete to look at him.

"You heard me," Pam said. "I'm pregnant." She paused for the briefest of seconds before adding, "And it's not yours. I had an affair with Bill, the lead anchor at the TV station. It's his."

"What?" Kevin gasped. "It's not even mine. Why you little slut. You whore!" he screamed. "That's right, I said it. You're nothing but a fucking whore!"

Pam's mouth dropped open in shock and amazement. She raised her right hand to smack Kevin, but as the arm came down, Dodger was there, stopping her.

"Whoa there," he said. "Now I think the bomb that was just dropped on Kevin's head was good enough for now. You don't need to hit him, too."

"Fuck off, Dodger," she snapped. "This is none of your concern."

"Well, I'm making it my concern," he replied, then locked eyes with Kevin. "Why don't you go and get our stuff from the chopper; let her cool off a bit. Hell, you too for that matter," he said at seeing how red Kevin's face was.

"That sounds like a good idea," Kevin said. "If I stay here I don't know what I might do."

As he walked away, Pam flipped him off. "Oh, big man, talking shit," she yelled at his retreating back. "You're all talk, Kevin, you know that? I dare you to try something. You ever hit me and it'll be the last thing you do."

"Screw you, bitch!" Kevin yelled as he climbed up the ladder to the roof.

"One big happy family, yes we are," Pete said as he sucked down desert, which was a jar of mushed bananas.

"Just ignore him, Pam," Dodger said. "He's angry. You can't blame him though. You cheated on him and got knocked up by another guy. Shit, anyone would be angry at that kind of news."

Pam sighed, some of her anger deflating. "Yeah, I know that, Dodger, it's just that the way he yelled at me, judging me. I don't need him to tell me I fucked up, but shit, in the end I'm still pregnant."

"You wanna get rid of it? I know how. Just find me a bottle of whiskey, a rag, and a coat hanger and we'll get that little fucker outta there real quick."

She blinked in horror at his suggestion. "You'll do no such thing. I'm going to have this baby and no one's going to stop me either."

Dodger held up his hands in surrender. "All right, all right, it was just an idea, no reason to go all psycho on me."

"It's probably her hormones," Pete added as he stepped up to them. "Women get crazy when they're pregnant."

Pam raised both hands and flipped off both troopers, one middle finger for each of them. "Fuck you, and fuck you," she snapped, then walked away to be alone.

"Women, am I right?" Pete asked, raising his own hand for a high five.

Dodger stared at the raised hand, then at Pete's face. Dodger shook his head, the gesture saying how pathetic Pete was acting, then he too walked away, wanting to find Kevin and see how the chopper pilot was doing.

Kevin was just coming down the ladder after getting some of their gear from the helicopter. As he dropped down to the floor, Dodger said, "You all right, man?"

"Yeah," Kevin replied. "I'll be okay."

"She says she wants to keep it," Dodger explained. "The baby I mean."

"Yeah, I bet she does. She told me once she wanted to have kids, I guess she just meant not with me." Kevin sighed. "Is it fucked up that I still love her? Even after what she's done?"

Dodger patted Kevin's shoulder. "No, man, it's not. Love is like that. Someone you love can shit all over you and you still smile and say, 'Can I have some more, please.' "

"Yeah, I guess you're right," Kevin said. Then he changed thoughts, wanting to focus on other things that didn't involve his love life. "Listen, Dodger, when I was on the roof I began thinking about some stuff."

"Like what?"

"Well, I was looking in some of the skylights, seeing the mall down there, and all the shit in the stores."

"Yeah, and?"

"Well, sure there are zombies in the mall but there are no living people, at least I didn't see any. So if we could kill all the zombies, we could have the entire mall for ourselves." He raised a hand to stop Dodger from speaking. "No wait, hear me out on this, I've really given it some thought. We don't have a lot of fuel left and who knows if we'll find more. I know I don't want to be walking around on the ground if we don't. But we got ourselves a good thing here, or we can make it a good thing. Think about it. All that shit down there, just ripe for the taking. Food, clothes, and weapons if they have a gun store. We can have it all for ourselves. Then, later, when things cool off and the zombies are all put down, we can go back to the city." He nodded that Dodger could talk now.

"I don't know, man. I mean, sure, we dropped into the mall for a bit, but we were gonna leave again, fly away on a new adventure. But now you wanna stay here? Shit, hasn't that been done before? I don't want to just retread someone else's shit. What's next? We go to a Walmart and hang out there?"

Kevin blinked. "What the hell are you talking about? What's a Walmart?"

"Huh? Oh, sorry, Kevin, I was thinking out loud. Yeah, I guess you're right. As long as everything we do is different from anyone else, we can do what the fuck we want here in the shopping mall."

"Ah, okay, sure, I guess so," Kevin said, not really understanding Dodger one bit. Had the trooper cracked under the pressure of it all? Had the man lost it and Kevin hadn't even seen it coming.

"Good, then it's settled. We're staying." Dodger turned to go find Pete, and then Pam. "Let's go tell the others the good news."

Chapter 8

Pete, Kevin and Dodger walked down the dark stairwell that led from the section where they had first arrived in the shopping mall. Behind them, at the door that led into the office space, Pam stood watching the three men depart with her hands on her hips, her jaw jutting outwards, her face set in a stern look of distaste.

The men had asked her to come with them but she had flatly refused. The last thing she wanted to do was traipse around the shopping mall with zombies everywhere. So she had stayed behind, while the men went out to investigate. They reminded her of cavemen, going off in search of food, while she remained behind in the cave to cook and clean.

Though things changed, in many ways they stayed the same, she thought. Closing the door and locking it, she went to the jars of baby food, opened one, and began to eat, while the men's footsteps, echoing outside in the stairwell, faded away.

Dodger was in the lead with his flashlight, the tight beam bouncing up and down as the trooper made his way down the stairs. His rifle was in his hands. Pete held his rifle as well, and the only one not holding a gun was Kevin.

Dodger had tried to give him one but Kevin had refused. He didn't know how to shoot and no doubt would end up shooting himself instead of his intended target. But the first chance he got in the mall, he planned on grabbing something to use as a bludgeon.

"Shit, it's dark in here," Kevin said.

"It should be better once we get into the mall itself," Dodger said. "The skylights will let some natural light in."

"Yeah," Pete added, "but then we have to deal with all the zombies."

"Nah," Dodger said as he stepped off the stairs and onto the bottom landing. "We can take them all out easy with these." He held up his rifle. "They won't stand a chance."

"Once we get set up we need to find a generator," Kevin said. "Then we can have power when we want it. I figure if we vent the exhaust through the broken skylight we'll be fine."

"Should be something in the hardware section of the Sears at the far end of the mall," Dodger suggested. "We'll get that later though. Right now I got my sights set on some fine cheeses and some expensive booze."

"I don't care what we get," Kevin said. "As long as it's not baby food it's okay with me."

"Aww, that stuff isn't so bad," Pete added. "I didn't mind it too much."

"There's a surprise," Kevin said, rolling his eyes.

Pete ignored his jibe. "So you want to live up there?" he pointed to the stairs leading to the offices. "Why don't we just find someplace nice in the mall once we kill all the zombies?"

Dodger stopped at the door leading into the mall. It was gray with a roll bar in the middle that would open it. "Because, stupid, if we set up in the mall and we get attacked or some shit from oh—I don't know—let's say a gang of bikers showed up. Then wouldn't it be a good idea if we weren't in the mall itself, but in some rooms that were out of the way?"

Pete gave that some thought and then nodded. "Sure, I guess. But what are the odds that a gang of bikers is gonna show up here? I mean, there's so many places someone could go for stuff, why come all the way here and then have to deal with all the zombies?"

Dodger considered Pete's words, and he had to agree that the black man made sense. "Shit, I guess you're right. If this was a movie that would be one hell of a coincidence that bikers showed up after we get the place all cozy and secure." He shrugged. "It's a good thing this is real life and not some cheesy movie." He cracked the door an inch. "Now both of you shut up so I can hear what's out there."

"I didn't say anything," Kevin said.

"I said shhhh," Dodger hissed and Kevin frowned; he didn't like being spoken to like a child.

Peering through the crack in the door, Dodger counted ten zombies moving through the gloom-filled hallway, looking like living shoppers who were window shopping. Their glassy-eyed stares made them look far too human for his liking.

Closing the door, Dodger turned to Kevin and Pete and said, "I count a dozen or so of them. That's four to one odds. Kevin, you hang back and let Pete and me take care of them. If one gets past us you can uh…"

"I can run away, Dodger, that's what. Unless I can get a club or something, I'm not fighting shit."

"Fair enough." Dodger said. "Our first priority will be to get you something to fight with. Maybe a baseball bat or a crowbar." He glared at Kevin. "But later I'm gonna teach you how to shoot so you can carry a gun."

"Fine with me," Kevin shrugged.

"Okay, Pete, you go left and I'll go right and we'll take down the ones out in the corridor in no time. You ready?"

"Yeah, man, let's do this," Pete said, raising his rifle.

Dodger slipped his flashlight into a pocket on his uniform, then with a nod to Pete, followed by another to Kevin, he threw open the door and charged out into the hallway.

As soon as the fire door was thrown open, the zombies turned as one group upon hearing the sound, then began to shuffle towards the two men.

The ones in front didn't get far, as Dodger began to shoot them consecutively in the head. Pete was right beside Dodger, following the senior trooper's lead, and in no time, more than a dozen zombies were down, spread out across the once-polished tile floor.

But as the troopers moved deeper into the corridor, a few zombies tried to slide past them, wanting to reach the fire door and what they thought was a way to escape the mall they'd been wandering in for more than a week, since the crisis began.

Pete swiveled on his right foot and shot the zombies trying to get past him, then he turned to face forward again and focused on the large mob of undead before him. What he didn't realize, as he hadn't taken the time to be sure, was that one of the zombies had only been only received a glancing hit in the temple, and it was already getting back to its feet. Pete and Dodger were a dozen steps from the door, where Kevin had been peering out, and now Kevin fell back in surprise when a pale, bloody face appeared before him. As Kevin retreated into the stairwell, the zombie followed.

Kevin retreated until his back was against the painted cinder-block wall. As the zombie moved closer, Kevin now sorely wished he'd taken that gun from Dodger when it had been offered. Even the chance of shooting his foot would be better odds than he was dealing with now. Kevin's eyes darted back and forth, seeking something he could use as a weapon, but the only thing in the stairwell was a fire extinguisher to his left. Out of options, and knowing if he didn't defend himself he'd be dead, he lunged to the side and grabbed the bright-red fire extinguisher, just as the zombie reached for him. Its hands slapped the cold concrete and it swiveled and came for Kevin again, something deep in its dead brain telling it that the prey would soon be caught.

Pulling the pin in the handle free with his left hand, Kevin held the extinguisher firmly with his right hand, then dropped the pin and took hold with his left hand, too. As the zombie came for him, its mouth open wide, Kevin leaned forward and jammed the nozzle into the open mouth. Squeezing the gun-like a trigger, the foam in the canister shot out of the nozzle and into the zombie's mouth. At first not much happened, though the sound of the foam flowing through the short hose was apparent, but then the zombie's eyes began to bulge, the cheeks having already puffed up, making the ghoul look like a squirrel storing nuts in its cheeks.

Kevin kept up the pressure, feeding more foam into the pale face, until finally, the head could take no more, and the eyes popped out, each one bouncing around the stairwell like ping pong balls. Foam shot out of every hole in the zombie's head: nose, eye sockets, ears and back out of the mouth and around the nozzle.

As Kevin stood still, holding the nozzle, the foam shooting outwards in all directions from the head, the skull began to swell up, growing larger, and then, before Kevin's eyes, the entire skull popped like an overfilled balloon, spraying foam and brains in all directions. Kevin was splattered with gore and bloody foam, and as it struck his face, he tasted bile in the back of his throat. The headless body of the zombie went slack and it slumped to the floor, dead. Kevin retracted the nozzle, feeling satisfied with himself despite the mess.

The door behind him leading into the mall suddenly banged open and he spun around to see Dodger and Pete standing there.

"You all right, Kevin?" Dodger asked upon seeing Kevin covered in gobbets of brains and red foam. As he stepped into the stairwell, his left boot came down on one of the eyeballs. It squished under the sole of his boot, squirting a pinkish-white mucus across the floor. Kevin felt his stomach heave a little at the sight and the sound of the eye being crushed, but he managed to keep from vomiting. If he wasn't going to puke after getting sprayed with brains, a squished eye wasn't going to be his undoing. Besides, he did good here, and didn't want to ruin it by vomiting before the two troopers.

"Yeah, I'm fine," Kevin said and gestured to the gore covering him. "None of this shit is mine; it's his," he said, pointing to the fallen zombie. Pinkish foam was still seeping out of the neck from where it had gone down the zombie's esophagus.

Dodger nodded, glad to see Kevin was unharmed. "Okay, we took out the one by the door but there are more coming. Now we need to secure the glass doors at all the entrances, that way no more can get inside."

"Count me in," Kevin said, "But I changed my mind about a gun. I want one."

Dodger pulled his sidearm and handed it to Kevin. "About time you came to your senses."

"Just don't shoot me with it," Pete added.

"I won't," Kevin replied. "Unless I have to."

Pete was going to ask just what Kevin meant by that when Dodger stomped back to the fire door. "Okay, guys, follow me. Let's take this place back from the zombies."

With Dodger in the lead, the three men began walking down the north corridor. The mall was like a cross, with a main area in the center, and the four arms of the cross each branching out to where there were glass doors to exit and enter. Here, zombies stumbled back and forth, many pushing the doors open.

Most of the stores had the metal grates down over their fronts, which was good, as no zombies could enter the stores, which would make finding them even easier.

Dodger and Pete did all of the shooting, taking down body after body as they moved along the hallway. Kevin followed behind, the gun in his hand, though he didn't really want to use it. Still, it felt good having it in his possession. As he walked, Kevin wiped the gore and foam from his face with his sleeve, but making sure to use a portion of the sleeve that wasn't already covered in gore. He wanted a shower badly, but he knew it would be a while before that option would even be possible.

As Dodger walked and shot zombies, his eyes flicked back and forth to the stores he passed. "Oh man, I can't wait to get into some of these places," he said as he passed a video rental store with more porn than actual legit movies.

"Tell me about it," Pete added as he walked by a store dedicated to nothing but candy. Shelves lined the walls on all sides with brightly-colored sugary treats, such as gummy worms and different kinds of chocolate. Pete found himself drooling, and he wiped his mouth, glancing to the side to make sure Dodger hadn't seen him. Dodger hadn't, the man focusing on shooting the zombies as they popped up from around shrubbery or kiosks located in the center of the corridor.

There was a large crowd of undead at the main doors, and Dodger and Pete got to work, blasting heads and punching and kicking any that got too close before getting shot.

"Get the doors, there's slide locks on the tops and bottoms of the doors!" Dodger yelled as he fought to push the zombies back. There were two sets of doors, an outer set and an inner set, the section between them used as a wind break. The zombies were packed pretty tight in the wind break, and Dodger and Pete shot heads like they were at target practice. Bodies fell to the floor, but that only complicated matters. With so many prone bodies on the floor, the troopers had a hard time walking, and reaching the outer doors.

Dodger used the butt of his rifle to shove a zombie away, then he locked the door before him. But as he went to pull it closed, a head darted forward, and the mouth on the pale face opened wide. Before Dodger could stop it, the zombie took a bite out of his wrist right where he'd been bitten earlier. The trooper cried out in pain. Dodger pried the teeth off him and shoved the face away and back out the doorway, then slammed the glass door closed, sliding the upper lock only. He could do the bottom one later, once the doors were secured. His wrist ached and bled bright droplets of blood but he had no time to deal with it now. He had to get the doors locked. He couldn't believe his luck, to be bitten not once but twice—and in the same damn place!

"Dodger, you all right?" Pete called; he'd heard Dodger cry out in what sounded like pain or surprise.

"Yeah, I'm fine, just had a close call is all."

More shooting and fighting ensued, but in a few minutes all the outer doors were locked, followed by the inner ones.

"We'll deal with the bodies in there later," Dodger said, gesturing to the corpses in the wind break. "But we still have three other entrances to lock down."

"Bring it on," Pete said as he popped in a fresh magazine into his rifle.

"I'm ready," Kevin said.

With Dodger in the lead, the three men moved down the now-empty corridor. Dodger inspected his new wound as he walked. The others couldn't see him, both men at his back. He was relieved to see the blood had already stopped and the wound wasn't that deep. The zombie had only managed to get two teeth into his flesh, and the wound wasn't much worse from when the last zombie had bitten him, and the other zombie had only scratched his skin. His arm was sore but he knew he'd live.

The next set of doors was slightly easier, with fewer zombies to deal with, and the last two were even simpler, given that it was mostly at the back of the mall and there weren't many zombies there, as they had congregated near the front. The ones that had been inside the mall were also swiftly taken down, until bodies lay everywhere in the corridors; heads blown apart, limbs hanging by threads from where bullets had all but severed the limbs from bodies. It had been a massacre, and the three humans were the victors.

When the last door was secured, the three men went to a bench in the corridor and plopped down, each breathing heavily from the exertion of battle, and sweating profusely from head to toe. All were covered in blood splatter.

"Well that was fun," Dodger said as he stretched out his legs.

"Yeah, but it's done now and this place is ours, man," Pete said with a wide grin. He could already taste the candy.

Dodger glanced at Kevin on his right, patting the man's leg. "You did good, Kevin, well done, man."

"Thanks, I did my best." Kevin had made a good showing, and by the time the men were on the last set of doors, he was shooting zombies like he'd been doing it all his life.

"We should get back to Pam and let her know the mall's ours," Kevin said. "I'm sure she's worried after hearing all the shooting." Really, he wanted to talk to her about his blowup. They had a lot to talk about actually, that is if he could keep from losing his cool.

"Aw, lighten up, man," Pete said. "She's fine."

Dodger was looking around, at the stores, the kiosks, finally taking in the mall more like a customer than a ransacker. "Wow, this place is fantastic. Everything we need, all under one roof."

"Yeah, man," Pete agreed. "We got it made here."

Kevin crinkled his nose at the smell of the corpses. "We still need to clean this place up. These bodies will start to smell even worse than before now that they're dead for good."

Dodger stood up, stretching. "Yeah, but first I need a shower and something to eat. How 'bout you two?" Earlier, in the back of the last room where they were staying, Pam had found a shower stall, probably put there for managers of the mall.

"I could eat," Pete said.

"Huh, you can always eat," Kevin said with a frown.

"Hey, I got a high metabolism," Pete said in defense.

"More like a 'fat' metabolism," Kevin quipped in reply, then began to walk away. He was about ten feet away, and turning a corner into the main corridor, when he found himself walking right into a zombie—one that had somehow managed to avoid the massacre of its brethren. Before Kevin could do more than cry out in fear and panic, the zombie was lunging for him, attacker and victim falling to the floor, where the zombie's blood-drenched mouth began coming closer and closer to Kevin's face. Kevin's gun was knocked from his hand to slide across the floor, out of reach. The moaning, growling of the zombie only added to Kevin's panic as he desperately tried to keep the clacking teeth at bay. The foul stench of death washed over him, making him spit up bile as his stomach threatened to empty its contents.

Pete and Dodger were still sitting on the bench, talking quietly together. At first they didn't hear Kevin's call for help, but then Kevin managed to yell louder and both troopers looked at one another.

"Looks like Kevin's gotten into trouble again," Dodger said with a weary sigh.

"We gonna go help him?" Pete asked.

With another sigh Dodger stood up. "Might as well. He's the only one who can fly that bird on the roof. He dies and we're all stuck here. Besides, he's my friend, so I guess that should count for something."

Pete stood up as well. "If he's your friend, you don't seem too eager to help him."

Dodger shrugged. "What can I say? We're not really that good of friends. More of acquaintances really. Well, closer than that, but not too much. Shit, if I hadn't run into him by accident the other day I never would have got the invite to go with him in the news chopper." He began walking. "Come on, let's see what's up." But when Dodger turned the corner and saw Kevin on the floor with a zombie on top of him, he went into action, rushing to his friend's side. He never would have delayed if he'd known Kevin had been fending off a zombie, he just figured the man had slipped on some spilled blood or something.

Kevin didn't see or hear Dodger arrive; he was in his own world, one where a slavering zombie was trying to bite his face off. Then suddenly everything changed as a knife tip appeared, jutting out of the zombie's right eye. The blade was embedded up to the hilt on the back of the skull, and as Kevin watched, the other eye of the zombie went still and the body slumped on top of him, going limp. Then Dodger was there, his body shading what light was coming from the overhead skylight.

Dodger leaned over and grabbed the zombie by the back waistband of its pants with one hand, while the other snatched the collar of the corpse's shirt, and with a heave he tossed the body off Kevin. The body slid across the floor to come up against a statue of a man. It looked a little like Michelangelo's David, only this one had clothes on that were molded into the statue. Exposed stone willies didn't go over well in public malls, Dodger figured as he glanced at the statue. "Kevin, are you all right? Jesus, I didn't know what was going on, I thought you'd just slipped or tripped or something."

"I...I..." Kevin said but couldn't talk. He was in shock, the attack too much for him.

Pete arrived as well, and he stood there watching. He didn't know what to do so he did nothing.

Dodger knelt beside Kevin and helped the pilot sit up. "Can you stand?"

"I...I, sure, yeah, I'm okay, Dodger. I just need a second to catch my breath."

"Shit, man," Pete said. "You almost became zombie chow. Did that guy bite you?"

"I don't think so."

"You don't think so?" Pete repeated. "Shit, man, you either did or you didn't. Which is it?"

"Why does it matter so much?" Dodger asked.

Pete blinked, surprised that Dodger, who seemed to know everything and was the most competent trooper Pete had ever met, didn't know about a zombie's bite. "Shit, man, if you get bit you get sick and turn into one of them things. Everyone knows that. It's like a general rule or something."

"Well, I never heard that," Dodger replied.

"No, he's right, Dodger," Kevin said, not regaining his composure. "I heard the same thing. The zombies have something in their saliva or something. A bite spreads whatever makes them walk around though they're dead."

Dodger swallowed hard. "So you mean if you get bit, you die?"

Pete shrugged. "Sure, man, pretty much. It takes a few days I hear, maybe longer, I guess it depends on the victim, you know, their constitution and shit."

"Where exactly did you two hear this stuff?" Dodger asked, his face taking on a mask of concern.

Both Pete and Kevin shrugged.

"Here and there, right, man?" Pete asked, looking at Kevin.

"Sure, here and there. Look, I'm going back to see Pam," Kevin said, walking over and picking up his lost gun. "You guys coming or what?"

"Hell yeah, I'm coming," Pete said. "I want to wash up; then I want to go get something to eat that's not baby food. This place has so much food to eat I don't know where to start." The two men turned and began walking, but when Kevin realize Dodger wasn't with them, he stopped and looked back the way he'd come. Dodger was still standing where he was, not moving, his face serious. "You coming, Dodger?"

"Yeah, I'll be right there. I, uh, I want to make sure there aren't any more stragglers around. One of us getting attacked like that was enough. Better to make sure there aren't any more around," Dodger said.

"You want me to stay and help you?" Pete asked, also stopping when he found himself walking alone.

"No, Pete, I got it, you go back with Kevin," Dodger said, forcing a smile.

Kevin and Pete turned and continued walking, the two men talking animatedly together. They were both excited about having the shopping mall all to themselves.

When the two men were gone, Dodger went over to another bench and plopped down. Pete's words were in his head as he slid back his shirtsleeve and stared at the double-bite on his arm. "Shit," he whispered, his shoulders sagging, his head drooping low.

Chapter 9

The three weary men got cleaned up and had a brief meal of more baby food. But they didn't mind, for they knew it would be their last time. The shopping mall was theirs. All they had to do was dispose of the bodies that lay everywhere, and once that task was done, they could begin exploring their sanctuary.

"We need to make sure to wear gloves when we clean up all those bodies; we can get some at the hardware store I saw at the south corner," Dodger said as he finished off a jar of banana mush. He studied the smiling baby face on the side of the jar for a few moments before placing it on the floor, where it joined half a dozen others. He'd given it a long thought before, as he stared at the wound on his wrist. In the end he decided if he was going to die then so be it. He wasn't a man to worry over things he couldn't control, so he'd stopped by a CVS with the grate down but not locked, grabbed some medical supplies, cleaned up the wound and wrapped it in gauze, and had returned to the others with a smile on his face. In time, the showing of good cheer had rubbed off on him so that now he barely thought about the wound. Besides, he felt fine. If he was getting sick he couldn't feel it. He did have a runny nose, but he'd had that 'before' he was bit, so if he was coming down with a cold or the flu, getting bitten had nothing to do with it.

"I was thinking about the bodies," Kevin said. "I bet there's some kind of dollies or something similar at the loading dock. We could use them to pile the bodies on."

"But once we do that where do we put them all?" Pete asked. "Shit, man, there must be almost fifty of them down there, maybe more."

"Why don't you just push them outside?" Pam suggested from across the room, where she was flipping through an outdated magazine someone had left behind, perhaps a maintenance worker who had found the empty rooms as a refuge or a place to take their breaks. Kevin had filled her in on what had happened in the mall, and how the zombies had been put down, and the outer doors to the egresses locked on all sides

Dodger swiveled on his butt from where he sat on the floor, his back against the wall. "And how do you propose we do that?"

"Simple," she replied. "The back parking lot of the mall, where the loading dock is, isn't that full of zombies, and the ones there are spread out. Just open a bay door and push the dollies outside. Problem solved."

Dodger rubbed his chin, feeling the stubble there. "That could work," he agreed. "Yeah, that could work really well." He stood up. "Okay, there's no use putting it off any longer. Come on, guys, we have work to do."

"Aw, man, I just sat down," Pete whined.

"You can rest up once we're done. Those things are gonna stink to high heaven if we don't get them out of this place. The sooner we do it the better."

"What about me?" Pam asked. "I can help, too."

"Are you sure?" Dodger asked. "I mean, your ah, condition and all. That won't be a problem?"

She crossed her arms over her pert breasts. "I'm fine, Dodger. I'm pregnant, I'm not dying of cancer, and I'm only a few months." She gestured to her stomach. "Hell, I'm not even showing yet, well not really." There was the barest hint of a baby bump if someone knew to look for it.

Dodger held up his hands to stop her. "Okay, okay, you can come. I was just asking."

Kevin was the first one down the stairs that led to the mall. At the bottom, the zombie he'd taken out with the fire extinguisher was still there. The blood pool had congealed and flies had appeared. Without discussing it, Dodger got one end of the corpse and Kevin the other, and they dragged the body out of the stairwell and into the hallway, leaving it with the other corpses scattered about.

"Let's get to the loading dock first and see what we can find. Then we can start collecting all the bodies," Dodger suggested.

"Sounds like a plan," Kevin said, Pete nodding in agreement.

"While you boys do that, is it okay if I have a look around?" Pam asked.

Dodger gave her a shrug. "Okay, but watch yourself. I checked to make sure we got them all but still, you never know if one might be hiding somewhere."

"I can take care of myself," Pam replied, then walked away, making a wide circle around any corpse she had to pass by.

With the three men walking side by side, they headed to the loading dock.

"How're we gonna get all these grates open?" Pete asked as they walked by a drug store.

Dodger shrugged. "We can shoot the locks off. Not a big deal." He gestured to the long hallway before them, which led to the dock. "But one thing at a time. First we clean this place up, then we can have some fun."

Their eyes lit up as they passed each store. There was everything a human being could want. Movies on videos, magazine kiosks with books and every magazine under the sun, toy stores, food stores which sold rare cheeses and crackers, the candy store Pete had found earlier, and more clothing stores with so much clothes, shoes, and jackets that the four of them could never wear it all in one lifetime.

Upon reaching the loading dock, the men found it wasn't empty, with the exception of three zombies, all wearing mall maintenance uniforms.

Dodger took out two of them, stitching them from head to toe before finally shooting each one in the face, and Pete killed the third with a single bullet to the head, then the men explored the loading dock. In a large back room, they found what they were looking for. Just as Kevin had predicted, there were half a dozen flatbed carts. The worn and battered dollies were six feet long and four feet wide, the paint faded and scraped.

"Well, guys, let's get to work," Dodger said and wheeled one of the dollies into the main section of the loading dock, positioning it so that he could push it through the wide, faded-brown door that led into the actual shopping mall. Kevin and Pete did the same, until all six dollies were lined up, as if they were staging them like cabs waiting for fares at the airport.

"We'll get these three last," Dodger said and pointed to the three prone, bullet-riddled bodies.

While the men got to work, Pam explored the shopping mall. As she peered through the metal grates, she had to admit she was looking forward to getting her hands on some of the items.

When she reached a section of clothing stores, she window shopped as she strolled along the empty corridor. Of course, bodies were everywhere, as well as pools of congealed blood and flies, and she had to constantly meander around the corpses while she walked.

Before she realized it she found herself at one of the entrances. The entrance was filled with bodies, all pounding on the outer glass doors. She walked closer, more than a little curious. It was like she was at the zoo, with the wild animals on the opposite side of the glass. When she was right at the inner doors, she stared out at the pale, bloody faces of the living dead. Pity welled up within her as she stared at the zombies. These had been people once, and now they were nothing but empty husks.

Looking behind her to make sure she was alone, she felt a little flirtatious, and before she realized what she was doing, she raised her shirt and flashed the zombies, pressing her breasts up against the glass. The surface was cool and her nipples became erect almost instantly.

"Peek-a-boo, boys," she said to the male zombies. There were females there too of course, but it seemed there were more men than women.

She began dancing back and forth as the zombies watched her, scratching at the glass doors, wanting to get in and attack her. She imagined they wanted to rape her, and she closed her eyes and fantasized how it would feel to have all those men touching her. It had always been a fantasy of hers to be taken by multiple men, but then it was just a fantasy, nothing she'd ever planned on acting on. She wasn't a fool and knew rape was anything but sexy. Perhaps she just wanted to be dominated by a man. Kevin wasn't the domineering type and again and again Pam found herself taking the reigns of their relationship, whether it was where they were going for dinner or in their bed. Just once she wanted to lay back and let the man take charge, to make the decisions, to tell her what to do. Of course she could never admit that, to anyone. What would all her girlfriends say? The ones who believed in equality for women, their feminism almost a living thing in itself. But then again, all her girlfriends were probably dead or hiding somewhere—just like her.

She was so focused on the zombies before her that she didn't see the one walking up behind her. The man had been a Jehovah's Witness in life, and the pamphlets he'd carried were still in a bag hung over his shoulder. Other than the bloody tear in his throat, and the blood that had spurted out to coat his shirt, he didn't really look that bad, well, considering how many of the dead that were about looked.

The dead man wore glasses, ones that were still affixed to his face, though they were slightly askew. His hair was thinning and he had a cold sore on his upper lip.

The first inclination Pam had that someone was behind her was when she felt a hand touch her shoulder, as if one of the men she was with was simply touching her, wanting to get her attention. So she turned around lazily, not expecting danger.

But instead of seeing Kevin or Dodger, who she expected to now have to give an explanation for her strange actions, she stared at the pale face and blank eye of one of the dead. Her mouth fell open in shock and she fell back against the glass door she had only moments ago been pressing her breasts against in a playful manner with the zombies.

The Jehovah's Witness moved forward, reaching out to grab her, his hands going around her throat and squeezing. Pam's tongue popped out of her mouth and her eyes became as wide as dinner saucers as white spots flashed before her vision. A wave of weakness, dizziness and nausea flooded through her, and she wondered if she could cause herself to have a miscarriage simply from being filled with terror.

With one great heave of her arms, she managed to break the dead man's grip and shove him away from her. The Jehovah's Witness fell backwards, and almost tripped over a fallen body, but at the last second managed to right himself. He came back in for the kill within moments of being forced back.

Pam, though filled with terror and panic, was able to stay calm enough to do something she had learned in a defense class more than a year ago. One of her girlfriends had suggested they go. It was a class where a police officer showed the women how to defend themselves in an attack, such as a mugging or a rape. She now used that training to defend herself. So as the zombie came at her, she yelled out the way she'd been taught, and kicked the zombie square in the balls, her foot fitting quite nicely between the dead man's legs. She felt the impact of the top of her foot connect with the zombie's testicles, and then felt them rupture like small balloons, but the Jehovah's Witness could have cared less, and he didn't so much as slow down, despite having become a eunuch.

The dead man reached out for her again and she managed to dodge to the side. The zombie's blood-slick hands slapped the glass behind her, leaving blood smears on the glass. Pam tried to run away but the zombie grabbed her shirt as she went to escape. She was pulled back so that her head and shoulders bounced against the glass, making a dull ring that reverberated through the shopping mall. Pam was able to look down the long corridor that led to the center hub, and she saw no one there. If she was going to live through this, she would have to do it herself, for there would be no one to save her. Behind her, the zombies at the doors were going wild, wanting to reach her.

The Jehovah's Witness was pawing at her and she fought him off, his fetid breath washing over her. The lungs still worked though there was no need, and the air seemed to seep out of the zombie more than simply exhale like in a living person.

Moaning loudly, the dead man came at her again, his hands curled into claws to tear and rend her flesh. Pam defended herself, however, refusing to go down without a fight. It was more luck than anything else that caused her to trip over a prone body on the floor. But as she went down, screaming in fear, not understanding, the action caused the zombie to loosen his grip on her. Pam landed on the body she had tripped over and then rolled to the side, coming off the corpse and getting to her knees. When she realized she wasn't being attacked by more zombies, and that she had only tripped, it filled her with relief.

But the dead man was already coming for her yet again, and she jumped to her feet and ran a few steps away, then stopped. The zombie was walking towards her but was rather slow, and she saw that she had a few seconds to gather her wits. She could run away and tell the others what had happened, or she could deal with it herself.

Standing tall, and fixing her clothing, which was in quite a disarray, she looked around for a weapon she could use that would allow her to stay safe. At first nothing caught her eye, but then she spotted a small planter near a wooden bench. Going to it, she bent down and picked up the planter, then got up onto the bench so she was taller than the zombie. She waited as the dead man plodded excruciatingly slow towards her.

When the Jehovah's Witness was only a few feet in front of her, Pam raised the planter high over her head, and when the zombie was standing before her, his hands reaching out to grab her, she brought the planter down as hard as she could, right onto the dead man's head. The planter was heavy and it was a decent bludgeon; the zombie's skull didn't stand a chance. The dead man went down to the floor like a ton of bricks had landed on him, his head becoming flattened from the weight of the planter.

Pam had closed her eyes when she'd brought the planter down on the zombie, so she opened them to see her handiwork. The planter had cracked in half, spilling dirt across the floor, and right beside it was the head of the zombie, looking a hell of a lot like the planter, only instead of dirt spilling forth from its cracked container of a head, it was brain matter and gore.

Stepping down off the bench, she looked at the body. She was shaking in terror but besides that there was something else swirling around within her; a sense of pride at being able to take care of herself. It was she who had killed this zombie, not one of the men.

Though she said it more to bolster her courage than anything else, Pam muttered, "That wasn't so hard. I don't know what all the fuss is about." Wiping her hands on the sides of her pants, she turned and began walking back down the corridor. She wanted to find the others; she didn't want to be alone anymore.

Chapter 10

The sun was setting, the shadows growing longer, the shopping mall standing alone in the large area that was its property. Zombies still banged on the doors leading into the building, but the glass was thick and just hands and fists would never be enough to shatter the glass.

The parking lot behind the mall wasn't as busy as the other ones surrounding the building. To reach it a person had to walk or drive all the way around the sprawling structure, and even when the world was normal people wouldn't do that—not if they didn't have to.

The parking lot itself was filled with no more than twenty zombies, all spread out across the asphalt. There were a dozen cars and pickups scattered about, too, the owners either some of the zombies walking around the area or people that would probably never return for their vehicles.

It was relatively silent, nothing but a few birdcalls coming from the nearby trees that lined the lot to break the tranquility. The zombies themselves were quiet, most barely moving.

Suddenly, a loud rattling sound filled the air, and one of the loading dock doors was rolled up. Every zombie in the parking lot turned as one and began walking towards the shopping mall.

Then, one after the other, six dollies piled high with corpses was pushed out of the bay door. There had been a little over fifty zombies in the mall, all wandering around when Dodger and the others had arrived. Most had gotten in later, after turning into the living dead, but a few had probably died and turned within the mall, such as senior citizens who arrived every morning to go for walks.

The dollies rolled and bumped across the uneven pavement, one of them veering off and crashing into a light post; the corpses were flung off the dolly when it came to such a sudden halt. Arms and legs flapped about as the bodies tumbled to the ground, a few near the edge of the pile rolling a few times before coming to a stop.

One dolly veered to the left and rolled all the way to the far end of the lot, until it hit a car—that's where it stayed. The other dollies remained in a straight line, as if some unknown controller was steering them. Each one made it to the far end of the lot, and only stopped when they hit the stone barrier that lined the parking lot, separating it from the land beyond the shopping mall, and the chain-link fence that was hidden by the trees and shrubs planted there for just that purpose.

The zombies that were in the parking lot barely made it ten feet before the loading dock door was pulled back down, the door hitting the ground with a loud bang. It would not be opened again.

Dodger turned to look at Pam, Pete and Kevin as he secured the lock on the door.

"That was easy," he said with a grin.

"I told you it would be," Pam replied. She was still shaken up from the incident at the mall doors a few hours ago, but she forced herself to keep it hidden. The men didn't need to know anything, and the entire time she had helped them clean up the bodies, she had remained silent. Kevin had asked her a few times if she was all right, and she had only nodded, saying she was just tired.

It had taken hours to clean up all the bodies, and it would take even longer to clean the blood and gore that shooting the zombies had created. But Dodger had assured everyone that the main job was getting rid of the bodies. The rest could be done at their leisure. While they had been collecting bodies, Dodger and Pete had taken a few extra seconds to blow off any locks on stores that needed to be removed. All across the shopping mall, the grates were up, giving the four survivors total access to its contents.

"It sure beats Pete's idea," Kevin said.

"Hey, putting all the bodies into one of the restaurant freezers wasn't that bad of an idea," Pete said, defending himself. He'd come up with the idea while they had been collecting the bodies, the reasoning being that it would be simpler to dump them in one of the freezers that belonged to the two large restaurants in the mall.

"Ah, yes, it was a bad idea," Pam said, holding up a hand and ticking off a finger at a time. "Number one; with the power off, those freezers are going to be rank from all that meat in there, and with dozens of bodies rotting in there, even the rubber seals on the doors won't help us contain the smell. Number two; there's still good food in there at the moment. It won't thaw out overnight, you know. We can cook a lot of it before that happens. And three, I don't know about you, but I don't want a freezer full of rotting bodies near me if I have a choice."

"Yeah, yeah," Pete said, "I get it. Shit, you'd think you planned on staying here indefinitely."

"And you didn't?" Dodger asked, butting in. "Shit, Pete, if things keep going like they've been out there…" He gestured to the world beyond the mall. "We might end up spending quite a long time here."

"I said I agree, it's done, can we not talk about it anymore?" Pete asked and walked to the door leading into the mall. "I think we're done here for now. I'm gonna get me something to eat, I'm starving." Then he was through the door and gone.

"What's his problem?" Kevin asked.

Dodger shrugged. "Who knows. Maybe he doesn't like thinking of being here for too long." He slapped Kevin on the arm and began walking to the door to the mall as well. "Why don't you and me see if we can find a generator and fuel, that way we'll have power in our new home."

"Sure, sounds good," Kevin replied. He glanced at Pam. "Will you be all right alone?"

"Yes, I'll be fine. I plan on grabbing a few things and then I'm going back to our 'new home,' as Dodger has aptly named it."

Kevin nodded and joined Dodger, who was waiting by the door, then the two men walked out into the corridor of the shopping mall. With Dodger in the lead, the two men began to explore, and finally found what they wanted at the back of a hardware store. There were five generators, all still in boxes. A little later still, in a small room where the maintenance workers stored their gear, they found a five gallon red plastic container full of gas. From what Dodger could discern, the gas was for snow blowers and the like, as well as the gas powered leaf blower and even a chain saw used to trim back the trees lining the mall's property.

They also grabbed a radio and some batteries so they could hear if anything new was happening in the city and the rest of the country.

When Dodger and Kevin returned to the office space with all they'd found, Pete was already there, gorging himself on candy, peanuts and cookies.

"Good, you're back," Pam said. "While you were gone I made a chart for cleaning the mall. We can get started tomorrow." On the wall, made of bright paper and drawn with colorful markers, Pam had made a chart and had put all their names in the boxes that assigned chores for each of them.

"Ah, yeah, that ain't gonna happen," Dodger said as he plopped down on the floor after he and Kevin had put the small generator down. He made a note that the next thing to get was some chairs, hell, maybe even a couch or an easy chair. He was exhausted. The cold or flu he felt was coming on was becoming worse. His entire body ached. But oddly enough, the wound where he'd been bitten twice was fine. He'd checked it and had put on some antibiotic cream before re-bandaging it. Then he'd found some antibiotic pills, and had taken two of those as well. Other than being a little sore around the edges of the wound, it was completely fine and was healing nicely. Absently scratching the bandage, as the wound was itching 'because' it was healing, he didn't realize he'd raised the sleeve of his uniform to scratch, and only realized it when he saw Pete staring at him, his eyes wide and locked on the bandage.

"What the fuck is that, man?" Pete asked, though Dodger had an idea Pete knew exactly what he was looking at.

"It's nothing. I cut myself earlier."

"Oh you did, huh?" Pete walked over and grabbed Dodger's arm. "Unwrap it. I want to see this *cut.* "

Dodger yanked his arm back. "No, it's a fucking cut, now drop it."

"No, I won't drop it." Pete turned to the others. "Guys, if Dodger got bit you know what that means. We need to know if he's gonna become one of them or not. Shit, just look at him. He's sweating and he looks paler than before."

Dodger stood up. "I've got the flu or a cold. I had the sniffles before I got bit. I'm not sick."

"Yeah, you are, you're turning," Pete replied. He moved so close to Dodger their noses were inches apart. "Let me see that wrist, now."

"Show it to him, Dodger," Kevin said, adding his voice.

"I have to agree with Pete and Kevin," Pam said. "If you've been bitten the rest of us have a right to know."

Dodger might have held his ground if only Pete had been challenging him, but with Kevin and Pam in on it as well, he decided there was no use denying it. "Fine," he said and began unwrapping the bandage. "But I'm telling you I'm not infected, I just have a fucking cold." The bandage came off and Kevin, Pete and Pam all gasped.

"See, I fucking knew it," Pete said, sounding self-righteous. "He's bit. He's gonna become one of them."

"Oh, Dodger, I'm so sorry," Pam said, tears welling in her eyes.

"Why?" Dodger asked. "I'm not going to die." He sighed. "I don't want to talk about this anymore. I'm gonna go find a couple of six packs and get drunk. I'll be back later." Without waiting for the others to respond, he turned and walked out the door, slamming it behind him. As his boots pounding the stairs faded, Pete turned to the others.

Pete shook his head sadly. "He's a goner; you guys know that, right?"

Kevin and Pam nodded.

"Well, he won't admit it but he will when he gets sicker. All we can do is be there for him, and when it's time, I'll do what has to be done." The fat trooper sighed.

"You're a good friend, Pete," Pam said.

Pete didn't reply, there was no need.

The radio crackled, static filling the air before the voice flattened out and became clear. "So, Doctor, you're saying there's no hope for mankind? That seems a little nihilistic," the reporter said.

"I have to disagree with you, sir," the doctor replied. His voice was haughty, academic. A man who wasn't truly aware of the real world, and only had life experience within the walls of academia.

"What we have here is nothing more than the Earth itself finding a way to cleanse the planet of a disease, namely us. Mother Nature has many ways to keep the Earth from becoming destroyed. Take cancer if you will. You see, humans are a parasite on this world and just like the Flood of biblical times, every now and then the slate needs to be wiped clean, so that the Earth can begin anew."

"So you're saying, Doctor, that this is the end of the world, that the dead rising is a way to wipe our world clean of people, so that the remaining survivors—if there are any—can start fresh?"

"Well, sir, you seem to have a grasp on most of it, but what you don't seem to fully comprehend is that I doubt there will be any survivors. You see, these dead beings feed on living people, and they can go anywhere people can go, so though it might take years to finally come to the eventual conclusion, sooner or later they *will* consume the population of the planet."

"And what happens to them once they do? What happens to the dead when they run out of food?" the reporter asked.

"Ah, yes, well, I would think as time passes they would simply decompose, just rot away, but in the end it doesn't really matter what happens to them."

"Why?"

The doctor paused, as if for dramatic effect, then said, "It doesn't matter, sir, because there won't be anyone left alive to care."

Kevin turned off the radio, having heard enough, as had the rest of them.

"Oh my God, could what that man said really come true?" Pam asked as she sat in a folding chair, one of a set of four, along with a card table and a lamp. The generator was in the next room, humming softly, the exhaust for it curling through the rooms and out of the skylight. A few lamps were scattered around the room, the soft light smoothing out the harsh tones of the stark room. Pam had planned on getting some more stuff the next day. Pete and Kevin, and later Dodger, had gotten the items they now had in the place. It had been decided that though they had the entire mall to themselves, to make their actual home up in the isolated offices was a better way to go. That way if there was ever any trouble, the helicopter was a level above them on the roof. Plus, if the mall doors were breached by the zombies, the added protection of the fire door at the bottom of the stairwell would mean that though the shopping mall would be lost, the four survivors would still be safe within their haven.

In a corner of the room were boxes of foodstuffs, everything from dried salami to specialty cheeses, to fancy bread and crackers. A small electric grill was in the far corner, and there was meat in a plastic tub defrosting, the meat having been taken from one of the restaurant freezers. Pam knew in a week, maybe less, all the perishables would be inedible, and would make a hell of a stink once they began to rot.

Dodger had gone to bed early after helping to get some of the furniture. Pete had immediately gotten on Dodger about his wound, saying he was tired because he was infected, but Dodger had adamantly told Pete he was full of shit. Then he'd gone off to sleep on one of the cots that had been brought up earlier. Later, when they were truly situated, the plan was to bring up mattresses, but for now the cots would suffice.

"Of course not," Kevin said, replying to Pam's question about the doctor's statement. "The guy's just talking shit. Saying what he thinks people want to hear."

"Who the fuck wants to hear that we're all gonna die?" Pete asked. He was chewing on a summer sausage, his mouth covered in grease.

Kevin looked at the fat black man, trying to remember a time when he hadn't seen the trooper eating something. And Pete wondered why he was so fat! *Stop eating for two seconds and maybe your weight will go down!* Kevin thought to himself. "I don't know, I'm probably wrong," he told Pete. "Maybe it's all just for ratings or something."

"Well, it's terrible," Pam added. "That guy needs a kick in the mouth for saying such things." She shook her head, disgusted. "I thought it was bad when I was at the TV station." She stood up. "I'm going to check on Dodger."

"Be careful," Pete said.

She nodded in reply, and walked into the next room, where Dodger was lying on his side, snoring softly. She knelt down beside him and touched his forehead. It was hot to the touch, and as she studied his face in the gloom, she saw he was sweating, though he seemed to have the chills at the same time. He didn't stir at all either, and his sleep seemed to be deeper than it should be. Not being a doctor, nor having much of a clue in the ways of medicine, she jumped to the conclusion that maybe he had fallen into a coma from the infection. She bit her lip in worry and returned to the others.

"Well?" Pete asked around a mouthful of sausage.

"He looks worse. I don't think he has much time."

"Shit, it must be spreading quickly. Okay, I'll stand watch over him tonight, you two just go about your business. I got this," Pete said, burping loudly, the odor of digested salami filling the air.

"I should be there, too," Kevin said, standing and taking a few steps towards the room Dodger was in. "He's my friend after all."

"Yeah, and that's why it should be me and not you," Pete said. He raised his revolver. "I'm gonna have to use this before morning. Could you do it? Could you shoot Dodger in the head?"

Kevin's face went blank as he considered it. "I...I don't know."

"Exactly man, but though I like Dodger, I'll do what has to be done." He wiped his mouth with the back of his sleeve and tossed the remaining summer sausage down onto the floor, on the wrapper it had come in. "Shit, it's not like there's a choice here."

"Go, do what has to be done," Pam said to Pete, then moved over to Kevin. "He's right, Kevin, he's trained for this sort of thing. Let him do it."

Kevin closed his eyes, weighing it all in his head. Almost a full minute passed before he did. "Fine, you do it." He extended a hand to Pete, who took it, the two men shaking. Kevin didn't even care that the chubby hand was so greasy that their shake was slippery and gross. "And thank you."

Pete shrugged, copying Dodger's frequent gesture. "Hey, someone's gotta do it; might as well be me."

In the next room, Dodger snored softly, unaware of his coming fate.

Chapter 11

Unknown to the others, Dodger had taken half a bottle of night-time cough medicine pilfered from one of the drugstores earlier before going to sleep, in the hopes of getting a good night's rest despite his cold. So he was totally out of it, the cold medicine making him oblivious to the outside world.

Across from him, sitting on the floor, was Pete. Between his legs Pete held his sidearm, the muzzle drooping to the floor lazily as he propped his arm with his knee. He wasn't very comfortable, and he planned on getting up and sitting in the folding chair he'd brought into the room, but for now he remained still, watching Dodger. Beside him was a pile of candy wrappers and soda cans from his vigil this night. A few feet away, a single Coleman lamp was on the floor, the light turned down low so as to bathe the room in shadows.

It was still a few hours before sunrise and he was tired. He'd managed to take a quick nap an hour ago but that was it. He didn't want to fall asleep too deeply and get caught unawares when Dodger died and reanimated. He knew it was coming; the only question was whether it was in an hour or two hours, or even three.

Pete stared at the lump across the room. Dodger was lying on his back, his face covered, almost as if he was already dead and someone had pulled the blanket over his head out of respect.

The body was perfectly still, and from Pete's vantage, it didn't even look as if Dodger's chest was rising and falling as the man breathed. As far as Pete was concerned, Dodger had succumbed to the infection and had died, only it had taken a day, not two or three.

In the other room, Pam and Kevin slept side by side in two cots pushed together. Whatever arguments they'd had were over, the two making up.

Pete stared at the inert form on the bed, his eyes riveted to it. Was there a twitch to Dodger's foot, or was it his imagination? He wasn't sure, and he focused his attention even harder on the still form hidden from view under the blanket.

There!

There it was again. A twitching of the right hand.

Pete sat up taller, the gun in his hand rising. He was psyching himself up inwardly, knowing what he was going to have to do in a few seconds. It was hard, harder than he thought it would be. Dodger had become his friend, and now Pete had to shoot the trooper in the head, then later he was going to bury the body in a small garden in the center of the shopping mall, near the fountain.

Pete stared in horror as Dodger slowly began to rise, the man coming up to a sitting position from the waist only. The blanket that had been covering his face slowly began to slide off. It was an infinite process, or so it felt to Pete. The blanket didn't just come off and then the face was visible, instead, it seemed to take its sweet time, hanging up on the brow, then the bridge of the nose, to then catch in the lips before coming free.

In the other room, Kevin farted in his sleep, the sound reminiscent of a fog horn. It broke the mood for a moment, and Pete looked to the doorway, as if he wanted to say, "Seriously? You fart now, at this exact second?"

Pam mumbled, "Pig," in her sleep, and the two were silent.

Pete turned back to Dodger, to see the man was now fully sitting up. His eyes were still closed, however, the body absolutely still—with the exception that he was now sitting up, of course.

Pete stared in fascination at the pale complexion, the drool coming from the corner of Dodger's mouth, the recessed brow.

A horrible stench filled the air and Pete assumed it was Dodger, his rotting corpse smelling up the place, but then he realized it wasn't Dodger but was Kevin's fart, which had wafted on the air currents and was now filling the room. Pete gagged at the odor, covering his mouth with his nose.

Dodger swiveled on the bed and slid his legs off the cot and stood up. Pete did the same, the gun coming up to put Dodger down for good. A low moan came from Dodger. It was similar to a yawn but longer and louder.

Pete leveled the gun at Dodger's head, and as he prepared to squeeze the trigger, he closed his eyes, not able to actually watch the bullet go into Dodger's head.

Dodger's eyes were still closed, and he turned to face Pete, his eyes popped open and he found himself staring down the barrel of a gun. The barrel seemed awfully large from his vantage point.

Pete fired the gun, and in the other room, Kevin and Pam snapped awake, both grabbing each other, and holding one another tightly, knowing what that fateful gunshot meant.

But instead of hearing nothing but silence, and only Pete still standing, they were shocked to hear Dodger yelling as high as he possibly could, screaming at Pete in unbelievable anger. They jumped to their feet together and dashed into the next room, to see a very alive Dodger standing a few feet from Pete, berating the surprised fat man.

"What the fuck is the matter with you, you dumb fuck?" Dodger yelled from the floor. When he'd seen Pete's finger on the trigger, he'd dived to the side, landed on the cot, then fell over it, all in the blink of an eye. Still, the bullet had come so close to Dodger's head that he'd felt the passage of it as the round split the air. If he'd been a micro-second slower in reacting, he would probably be dead right now.

"Oh my God, you're alive?" Kevin said in amazement, Pam repeating the sentiment.

Dodger glanced at them, his eyes wide in anger, his once pale complexion now red from anger as blood filled his cheeks. "Of course I'm alive. Why the fuck wouldn't I be? And why did this son-of-a-bitch just try and kill me?"

"I thought you were a zombie," Pete said, defending himself. "You were bit; then you died and came back. I did what I was supposed to do; I shot you in the head."

Dodger slapped his forehead with the palm of his hand, then did it a few more times, as if by doing this he could bang some sense into Pete's head through force of will. "How many fucking times can I tell you people, I was bit, yes, but I'm not sick."

"But you were so pale earlier," Pam said. "And you were so still, like you were in a coma."

Dodger sighed. "Maybe that's 'cause I took half a bottle of cold medicine so I could get some sleep. I had a head cold, which is gone I might add, though if Pete'd had his way, the head cold would never come back 'cause I'd have no fucking head for it to be in." He glared at Pete, his eyes seeming to glow with anger. Both hands were curled into fists by his side.

Pete wondered if Dodger was going to lunge at him and attack him. He looked down, studying his boots. "I don't understand it. You got bit, you were supposed to turn and then come back."

"You act like you're disappointed," Dodger said, then sarcastically added, "I'm so sorry I didn't die and come back—there, happy?"

"No," Pete said in a low voice, like a scolded child. "Of course not."

Dodger stepped up to Pete and slapped the man in the face, then took the gun from him. "You can have this back when I think you can handle it, and not before." He pointed to the doorway. "Now get out of my sight before I fucking kill you myself."

Pete looked at Kevin and Pam, then back at Dodger. "Why don't you yell at them, too. They thought the same thing, but it was me who had the balls to take you out."

"So what? You want a fucking reward? Maybe a pat on the back?" Dodger snapped. "Just go, before I change my mind and shoot you anyway. I could you know, self defense and all."

Pete stomped out. "It's not fair," he said to Pam and Kevin. "You thought the same thing."

"Sorry, Pete," Kevin whispered.

A few seconds later, the crinkling sound of Twinkies being ripped open filtered into the room. Pete was upset so he was eating.

"So you two thought the same thing, huh?" Dodger said to Kevin and Pam. "What the hell is wrong with you? Do you know how close Pete came to killing me? A fraction of an inch to the right and I'd be dead right now. And why? Because I had a fucking cold?"

"We're so sorry, Dodger," Pam said.

"Yeah, man, you don't know how sorry. But can I tell you how good it is to see you up and around? I mean, we thought you were a goner, and now here you are, looking fine and yelling at us."

Dodger could see the relief in their eyes and his face softened. They were glad to see he was alive; that had to count for something after all.

"Yeah well, I do feel better than yesterday. I guess that cold medicine did the trick." He flexed his arm where he'd been bit twice. "This feels better, too. I can't even feel any pain when I move my wrist."

"Thank God," Pam said. "I was so worried about you. Hell, we were all worried."

"Hell yeah," Kevin said and walked over to Dodger and patted his friend's arm. "I can't believe you're standing before me. When we heard the gunshot, well…"

"Let's not dwell on that," Dodger said, glancing behind him to look at the bullet hole in the wall. There was a small pile of plaster dust right below the hole on the floor. Dodger thought about what he would need to patch that, the items he would get from the hardware store in the morning. Then he changed his mind. Pete would get the stuff for him; after all, he'd made the hole.

Pam was asking him a question and Dodger came back to the here and now, saying, "Huh, what? Sorry, I was thinking about something."

"I said," Pam repeated, "why did you get up in the middle of the night anyway?"

Dodger gave that a brief thought and replied, "Well, if you must know, I woke up because I had to take a shit, but after Pete trying to kill me, I don't have to go anymore."

"You don't?" Kevin asked.

"No, I don't. But what I do need is a change of underwear."

"Is that smell coming from you?" Pam asked with a grin, and she wrinkled her nose a little. "I thought it was from Kevin, you know, one of his loud farts he insists on sounding off every hour or so in his sleep."

Dodger shrugged. "Maybe some of it is, but I'll tell you this, Pam. If you opened your eyes after a sound sleep to see a gun aimed at your head and the shooter already squeezing the trigger to fire, I'd bet you anything that you'd shit your pants, too."

Chapter 12

Time passed for the four isolated friends, weeks turning into months. What little information came from the radio, and in time that too ceased. The television was no help at all, and other than an Emergency Broadcast signal, there was nothing there. Most channels were only static, white snow that hissed and popped, hypnotizing a watcher until someone else broke the spell by turning off the screen.

The shopping mall was spotless, Pam doing most of the work cleaning all the blood and gore and bits of brain that had coated the glass walls of stores and the once-polished floors. Though she complained a lot, she really didn't mind, as it gave her something to do.

The men had target practice on the roof to keep busy. Kevin had become a decent shot, too. Pete was fatter than ever, the man spending all his time eating. He said it was his duty not to let the food spoil that wouldn't last too much longer.

All the men spent way too much time in the video store on the north side of the mall, especially the back room that was filled with adult video tapes. Pam had never gone in there but she'd heard the men talking once, how they'd set up a TV and a generator so they could watch porn. The funny part was though Kevin and she still had sex regularly, despite her being five or so months pregnant and showing more than a little, it was 'he' who went in there the most.

Pam had found all the maternity clothes she could ever wear in ten lifetimes in one of the department stores, and the clothes did a great job of hiding her belly. In a matter of months she would be giving birth and she didn't like thinking about the delivery, and how the men would have to help her. She'd decided weeks ago that she would deal with it when the time came, and that until then it was nothing but one more thing to worry about. Dodger had been reading up on baby delivery in books he'd gotten from the one large bookstore in the mall.

It was late in the day—what day it actually was unknown to her—and Pam was taking a walk around the mall, doing her daily exercises. She stayed away from the glass entrances, not liking the way the zombies stared at her like she was a three course meal.

The men were off doing something, and she'd frequently found that the mall had turned into a boys' club, one where she was of course not invited. Humming to herself, thinking about how easily she had adapted to her new life of basic luxury, as the mall had anything and everything she could ever want, she strolled down the lonely hallway of the second floor of the shopping mall, her gait becoming more of a waddle with each passing day. She was alone and she was happy about it.

Being cooped up with the men in the small office space they called home could become very irritating, and she needed some time to be by herself, to organize her thoughts about her life and future.

As if sensing her inner turmoil, the baby in her belly kicked, causing her to wince and smile at the same time. The young life was growing, and a few more short months would be all it would take to bring the new baby into the world.

An undead world.

Still, no one knew why it was happening, though suppositions and ideas had ruled the airwaves before they had faded almost all together. But the one thing that was true, was that the dead walked and they weren't going away anytime soon.

Pam, Dodger, Pete and Kevin, had resigned to live for as long as they could inside the massive shopping mall, while the world crumbled outside the brick and mortar walls. Thinking of the three men made her think of Dodger first, and how Pete had almost killed him months earlier. Dodger had been okay. He'd recovered from his cold and the wound on his wrist had healed just fine.

Pam sighed wearily as she strolled from store to store, staring at the best of today's fashions. All the metal grates were up and she had the entire building to herself.

She had left the men playing cards back in their makeshift apartment, the three gambling with thousands of dollars taken from one of the stores that had contained a small vault in one of the back offices. Of course, the money was worthless now, with the exception of perhaps as toilet paper or kindling for a fire.

As she walked, she tried to remember what the shopping mall had looked like when it would have been crowded: children with their mothers, the little ones complaining that they had to get clothes or shoes, old men and women out for a walk in the mall, fascinated by the massive building devoted to capitalism, to the almighty dollar.

But now they were all dead or walking around as zombies.

A chill went down her spine and she found herself cradling her belly, wanting to protect the young within her from the dangers of the world.

Of course, those dangers were now so much more than what they once were.

She slowed when she reached a small jewelry store, admiring the beautiful necklaces and pendants in the window. Inside the store proper, racks of earrings—gold and sterling silver the most predominate—glittered under the fluorescent lights.

Glancing over her shoulder and feeling like she was somehow doing something wrong, she stepped into the store to see what she could take.

The smell of wetness on cardboard tickled her nose and she looked for the source. Moving deeper into the store, she searched the floor and ceiling, and sure enough, at the corner of the ceiling, right over a door leading to the backroom, she saw a small water spot about six inches in diameter.

She smiled to herself as she brushed her now-long hair off her face. Even here, in a relatively brand new building, there were problems such as leaks.

Deciding she wasn't going to worry about it and would tell the men later, she began browsing, seeing what might catch her eye. The entire time she looked, Kevin was in the back of her mind as she wondered what he would like to see her wearing.

Another smile creased her thin but shapely lips as she thought of Kevin. He had actually asked her to marry him a while back, but she had turned him down. Without a ceremony, without a priest, it all seemed so hollow, and though Kevin was a decent boyfriend, she'd never really thought of him as 'marriage' mate-rial.

A set of solid gold, 14k earrings caught her eye and she placed them to her ears, admiring them in the small circular mirror on the counter. She felt rich as she admired herself but finally put them down, realizing whether the earrings were made of gold or simple iron, they were worth nothing now.

Monetary wealth was a thing of the past, and she knew she was one of the richest people still alive, with three good friends and a coming baby she could call her own.

Why was this? Why did she think this when outside the walls of the mall the world was nothing but zombies, that wanted nothing more than to kill and eat her and her unborn child?

Because she had safety, shelter and food. And lots of it, and in a world where the dead were looking for their next meal, that was all anyone could ask for.

She leaned against the glass counter, thinking about how her back hurt. Looking for a chair, she found one near the end of the counter. It was more of a stool, but it would do the job of getting her off her feet just fine.

Sitting down, she sighed, feeling the baby shift inside her. Even now, months later and used to being pregnant, it still fascinated her how an actual life could be growing inside her.

Pam leaned her head on the glass counter with her arms for a pillow and closed her eyes, thinking she would just rest for a bit. Then she would go back to the men and start supper.

Though she had once told them she wouldn't be their mother, that was exactly what she had become, and though Dodger would cook sometimes, usually it was just her.

Pam didn't mind, it gave her something to do. She'd changed since coming to the shopping mall, had grown up a lot. She had been a spoiled girl before the dead began to walk, but since then, Pam felt she'd turned into a woman, and one that knew how fortunate she was to be alive.

Closing her eyes, she sighed one more time, and though she wasn't planning on it, she drifted off into a light nap.

A tapping sound filtered into her dream of her running on a beach, the surf gently cascading over the rocks lining the shore. At first she didn't know what the tapping was, the noise flowing into her dream, but then she opened an eye, realizing the tapping was external.

Yawning and wiping the corner of her mouth where spittle had collected, she blinked up at the dark fluorescent lights, wondering if they would ever be turned on again.

But then she heard the tapping again and knew it was real.

Standing up, she felt a wave of dizziness and waited a moment for it to pass. Her waning strength was due to the baby; she knew this, and though Kevin hounded her to get some more rest, she usually didn't sleep much.

That was when the nightmares came and she thanked whatever god was up in the heavens for giving her a slight repast when she had slept on the stool here in the jewelry store.

Then she heard it again, the tapping sound, almost like Morse code. Not that she knew Morse code, but she had watched old Navy movies with Kevin on Saturday nights when they didn't feel like going out, and it sounded close enough.

Her ears tried to focus and she soon found herself looking at the door leading to the back room. She bit her lip nervously, trying to decide what to do.

She should go get the men; they would deal with whatever was back there.

But as the light tapping continued, she felt her nervousness abating. It couldn't be a zombie for one of them wouldn't be tapping like that. No, they were clumsy, hideous things that would never have the dexterity for something as gentle as tapping.

With a glance to the hallway outside the jewelry store, she decided she wanted to check it out on her own. Sure she was pregnant, but she wasn't helpless. She could still fight and shoot and do what had to be done. She knew the men didn't think that of her like that, but it was the truth. She thought back to the Jehovah's Witness zombie she'd killed back when she'd first arrived with the men at the mall. Yes, she could handle herself when it was warranted.

Besides, the noise was probably something simple. After all, the men had cleared the shopping mall of zombies months ago, and if there had been one still around, it would have been found by now.

For the zombies didn't lie in wait; they weren't that smart. They would have come out of hiding long ago in search of fresh meat.

So Pam took a step towards the backroom door, and with an intake of breath to strengthen her resolve, she entered the dark interior.

It was dark and even mustier in the back room, and she reached out to the wall near the door to see if she could find a light switch, then stopped, knowing there was no power. Even after all this time her instinct had been to reach for a switch.

Lowering her hand, she slid a hand into a pocket of her pants and pulled out a small penlight flashlight. All of them carried one. It had been Dodger's idea.

Flicking it on, the room was illuminated in the thin beam of light, the rest of the place where the beam didn't go still wreathed in shadow. Standing still, she waited to hear the tapping again. When more than a minute came and went and still no tapping, she began to wonder if she'd imagined it.

It was when she was ready to leave, to just forget the entire thing, that she heard it again. It was coming from her left, and with her curiosity peaked, she began to walk in the direction of the noise, her heart beating fast in her chest.

As she walked, her sneakers stirred up small dust bunnies, and a thick layer of dust was brushed aside. This told her immediately that none of the men had been back here for a long time, if ever.

She could see that though it was the backroom to the jewelry store, it was also part of another store, one that must have sold houseware items according to the boxes she passed. Many held Tupperware and silverware to name a few items.

Passing by piles of boxes stacked head high, she had a feeling of dread that maybe she should go back, that if the men hadn't cleared the back room properly, she would now be setting herself up for trouble.

The shopping mall had become her home and the comforting feeling of safety had dulled her sense of danger. The place was huge and it was possible a zombie could still be hiding within its walls, whether in the basement or in a back room somewhere; perhaps trapped by its own stupidity.

Just as she was making up her mind that it was time to leave, she rounded a corner and stopped cold, her mouth falling open in a silent gasp of fear. Standing in front of her was a zombie, wearing what looked like a security guard's uniform.

It wasn't hard for her to figure out the dead man must have worked for the shopping mall, and it was all too clear what the zombie was doing back here and what the tapping she had heard was from.

The undead security guard was handcuffed to a steel water pipe, and every time he pulled at the cuff, the metal handcuff would tap and scrape the pipe. How he had become handcuffed was unknown, but a hundred reasons came to mind, one being that a fellow worker had done it when the guard had turned.

At first Pam wasn't worried, and felt her heart slow at the sight of the handcuffed zombie. For if the zombie was attached to the water pipe, he was harmless and it would be simple to just go get Dodger and have the trooper put down the guard for good.

But it was either a coincidence, or simply that the sight of fresh meat made the dead man begin to pull harder, but the security guard yanked so hard that his arm popped out of the socket and the rotting meat stretched like aged elastic until it separated. All Pam heard was the ripping of what sounded like dry paper, then she saw that where the arm once stuck out of the blue shirtsleeve of the dead man's uniform, now there was just a missing limb.

But worse was that the zombie was free!

Before Pam could turn and run, the security guard was on her, knocking both of them into a pile of boxes. Pam yelped in terror as she was buried under the boxes, the zombie still on top of her. Using her hands, she jammed them under his slime-coated chin and felt the coldness of the dead skin. As she watched, her hands slid into the flesh, becoming buried in it, and she gagged on bile at the feeling.

But the zombie was only half of a threat, thanks to the one remaining arm, and Pam so far was managing well, but she knew with the baby inside her that she wouldn't be able to fend the zombie off for long. She didn't have the stamina of a woman who wasn't pregnant.

Quickly, her eyes began searching for a weapon, any weapon in which to protect herself and destroy the zombie trying to kill her and her baby.

Though she was terrified, she still wouldn't yell out for help. There was no point in doing so. Pam knew it would be a waste of time; the men were on the other side of the mall and wouldn't hear her, no matter how loud she yelled.

Removing one hand from under the zombie's chin, her arm began to flail about, her fingers touching anything that was around her. Her throat vibrated with her groaning exertions, and the zombie moaned and wailed right along with her. Teeth clacked only inches from her face, her nose seeming to be the preferred choice on the menu today. Turning her face away, she felt cold saliva drip onto her skin, causing her to want to vomit. Only her force of will kept her lunch inside her.

The zombie wasn't letting up. It had been trapped for months, and the sight of Pam was too much for it. Its entire world was only her, and it wanted her badly, only Pam's desperation keeping the dead man at bay.

Finally, Pam felt something smooth with a handle under her flailing hand. She grabbed it, not knowing what it was, nor caring. Pulling it to her, and then up and at the zombie's head, she saw that it was an electric carving knife.

Glancing to the floor where she had found it, she spotted dozens of them spread out, the box holding them open, the packing peanuts they were in scattered everywhere.

Never hesitating and thanking whatever good fortune was shining down on her today, she brought the immobile twin blades up and under the zombie's chin. Shifting the hand she still had on the zombie slightly lower, so her palm was now pressed against the guard's clavicle, she began to saw back and forth at the dead man's neck.

As Pam worked, cold and coagulated blood poured out of the jagged wound, mixing with the browns and blacks of what had to be blood, too. The viscous contents splattered down onto Pam's lower face and chest; she closed her mouth tight as well as her eyes, not wanting to get any in her mouth. But she didn't need her sight to finish what she'd started. Sawing back and forth, she felt the twin blades get stuck, becoming hung up on something hard; she had no idea that she'd hit the zombie's spine. Still sawing, her body covered in gore, she moved her arm back and forth with all her might, knowing she was growing tired.

Finally, after what felt like an eternity, the twin blades pushed free of the obstruction and there was no longer any resistance. Pam felt something fall onto her forehead and bounce off, to then roll away. The object hurt when it hit her head but the pain was only for a moment, then it was gone.

At first she did nothing, merely laid prone on the floor, breathing heavily from her exertion, ready for the zombie to try and attack again. But when the corpse remained immobile, she put the electric knife down and used her shirtsleeve to wipe her eyes clean of gore.

When she was confident she had cleaned herself enough to open her eyes, she gazed up at the headless security guard, a small amount of brown blood still seeping out of the jagged neck stump.

Pushing the corpse off her, Pam sat up and wiped her face some more, spitting as much as she could, and fearing the unknown. As far as any of them knew, a bite was supposed to kill you, even though Dodger had been okay. But what would happen if you got some tainted blood in your mouth? Was it saliva or something else? No one knew and she didn't want to find out the hard way, and though Dodger had been fine after being bit, if the same results would befall her wasn't worth the gamble.

Rolling to her side, she spotted the severed head on the floor a few feet away. It was lying on its left ear, and as she watched it, Pam saw that the head was still very much alive.

Standing slowly, as it was hard to get to her feet without help, she reached down and grabbed a towel draped over a box across the aisle.

Pam wiped her face and neck as much as she could and knew she would be heading directly for the shower when she was through here. But there was still one last thing to do before she left, and informed the men that she'd found a zombie, one they had missed.

Bending over, which was never easy when you were pregnant, she picked up the electric knife and walked over to the severed head. The eyes rolled in their sockets and the mouth opened and closed, but without a larynx, there were no sounds.

With the toe of her brand-new right sneaker, she tipped the head over, using the bottom of her sneaker to keep the pale features looking straight up at her. Then, using the electric knife like a dagger, she jammed it into the head's right eye socket.

The eye exploded and the socket began to ooze clear ocular fluid as the other eye began to bounce back and forth. It was hard to see this as a thick film of cataract had grown over the eye, but if Pam stared at it long enough, the dilated pupil could still be seen floating within a sea of milky white.

She twisted the knife in the socket, metal scraping on the sides of the socket, bone shavings joining the mix of gore, but the twin blades did their job, slicing the brain to pieces and killing the head for good.

Standing up, Pam dropped the electric knife to the floor, ignoring it when the casing cracked and pieces of plastic flew off. It didn't matter; it wasn't like she would ever use it to cut a ham or a roast taken from one of the voluminous freezers or walk-ins, as all the meat had long spoiled, and to even open the door of one of the freezers would unleash a stench so foul it would probably never leave the mall. She had peeked in once months ago and the entire freezer had been wall to wall maggots. She'd slammed the door closed as fast as humanly possible, then had vomited up her the entire contents of her stomach, as the odor had been so rank.

Gazing down at her handiwork, she didn't move for a few seconds, just glad to be alive. Her adrenalin was pumping hard, and the fight or flight was still there, only she had chosen to fight. Or had she chosen 'fight' because she didn't have a choice?

Her baby kicked inside her and she reached down and cradled her belly. Touching her extended abdomen, she was relieved to discover everything was fine. She hadn't been hurt in the assault, nor was the baby.

She knew this was true without a doubt.

A mother knows these things, she thought and then began to chuckle. Just imagining herself as a mother was still hard to contemplate.

Only months ago the most she had to worry about was the schedule at the television station and what she was going to have for dinner each night, and whether she should wear a black bra or no bra with her evening dress when she and Kevin went out on Friday nights.

With one last look at the decapitated security guard, she turned and walked away.

As she entered the front of the jewelry store again and passed by the glass counter, where she had put the gold earrings down, she paused and picked them up again.

Looking at them now, they took on an entirely new light for her.

"I earned these," she said to herself, knowing the earrings would always be a reminder to what had happened here today. But best of all, it would remind her of how she had triumphed, by herself, with only her wits to get her by—just like she had done with the Jehovah witness zombie months ago.

That made her think of how easily any one of them could be killed. If Kevin was killed then the helicopter on the roof would be worthless, as the rest of them didn't know how to fly it.

That made her think some more, about how it wouldn't be a bad idea that one of the others learned how to fly. She decided it would be her.

The next time she saw Kevin she would tell him her idea, and if he balked, she would keep at him until he finally gave in. She would learn to fly the helicopter, and then she would have something more to contribute to the group other than cooking and cleaning.

Squeezing the earrings in her palm, she grinned from ear to ear, then pleased with her coming plans, Pam walked out into the hallway and down to the main gallery, then back to the offices she called home with the men.

There was a shower with her name on it, and that too, she had earned.

Chapter 13

While Pam had an adventure in the back of a jewelry store, Dodger, Pete and Kevin had gone up to the roof of the shopping mall for some target practice after playing cards.

"Got him," Dodger said, shooting a tall zombie in the head, one of more than three hundred wandering around the grounds of the mall. When the helicopter had first arrived and landed on the roof, no more than a hundred zombies had been around the mall, but as time passed, more had appeared, until there was now a vast mob of undead on all sides of the massive building.

Behind the three men, lying near some A/C ductwork, was the severed head that Pam had kicked away from her upon first arriving, after Dodger had tossed it up through the broken skylight.

The head was now quite desiccated, the mouth barely moving. Both eyes were gone, as was the tongue, the soft tissues eaten long ago by crows and other carrion eaters that flew.

In all that time, no one had come; not law enforcement, nor people seeking to raid the mall for its valuables, or more survivors looking for a place to hide from the dead. No one had come, that in itself telling the four lone friends what was happening in the world outside the mall.

"There, shoot that one," Pete said. "The one that looks like Doris Day." Dodger found the woman that Pete was pointing to and a second later the zombie's head was exploding as the round blew apart her skull, splattering nearby zombies with blood, bone and brain matter.

The parking lot was riddled with fallen bodies from past kills, some nothing more than skeletons thanks to the rats and other critters that fed on dead flesh. The rodents darted to and fro, feeding on the dead flesh, gorging themselves.

"Okay it's my turn," Kevin said, and Dodger handed him the rifle.

"Remember, Kevin," Dodger said. "The sight is a little off so you need to compensate for that."

"I know, you've told me before," Kevin replied, annoyed, then he lined up a pale face in his gun sight and fired. Only the top of the scalp was taken off the zombie's head, making it look like a reverse Mohawk.

"You missed," Pete said flatly.

Kevin looked away from the gun sight and at Pete. "No shit, I missed. I didn't compensate like I was supposed to."

"Why not?" Dodger asked. "I just told you to…"

"I know, I know," Kevin snapped. "Jesus, give me a second already. I can do this." He lined up the face of the zombie again, let out the breath he was holding, and squeezed the trigger. This time he did compensate for the gun sight, and across the distance, the zombie's face imploded from the impact of the high velocity round, after which the back of its head was blown outwards, brains flowing out like an air hose had been jammed into the zombie's nose and turned on.

Kevin lowered the rifle and smiled. "See? I told you I could do it. You taught me well, Dodger."

"Fuckin' A," was Dodger's reply. Of course he'd taught Kevin how to shoot well.

Pam's head popped up through the broken skylight, though it wasn't really broken anymore. A plastic piece with a hinge had been put there so that it could be opened and closed easily, yet keep the rain and cold out.

"Kevin, I need to talk to you," Pam said. Her hair was still wet from her shower. As soon as she'd cleaned up she'd gone right to the roof skylight, wanting to share her ideas with Kevin on learning to fly.

"Shit, what's she want?" Kevin said to Pete and Dodger, rolling his eyes, as if to say, *Women, they never leave you alone.* Kevin handed the rifle back to Dodger. "I'll be right back."

"Take your time," Dodger replied and lined up a zombie down below, blowing the head clean off its shoulders, Pete yelling in surprise when the skull exploded like a watermelon stuffed with dynamite.

Frowning at missing out on the fun, Kevin walked over to Pam, who was still at the skylight. She wasn't planning on climbing all the way onto the roof. She stood on a sturdy ladder found in one of the stores. The one once used was long gone, replaced by the better model.

"What do you want?" Kevin asked flatly.

Pam quickly explained her thoughts on learning to fly, and her reasoning if Kevin was killed. Kevin listened with a set jaw, then finally shook his head no.

"Why not?" she demanded.

"There's a dozen reasons," he said. "But the main one is we're low on fuel. I don't want to waste it teaching you how to pilot my baby."

"But if you get killed, no one will be able to fly the damn thing," she rebutted.

Dodger had overheard some of the conversation, so he walked over, joining them. Pete stayed at the edge of the roof, taking shots at the zombies.

"She has a point, man," Dodger said. "You die and we're not leaving by that chopper."

"Then I'll teach *you* how to fly," Kevin told Dodger, who shook his head no.

"Nah, would be a waste of time. I don't like to fly."

"But you were fine when we came here," Kevin said.

Dodger shrugged. "Sure, but I hated every minute of it. Besides, it wasn't like I had a choice. It was the best way out of the city." He pointed to Pam with his chin. "Let her learn. She wants to and it'll give her something to do."

"Sure," Pam said, glad Dodger was on her side. "I can read up on how to fly too, there's tons of books in the bookstore about it. Then after I've studied, you can show me the real thing."

Kevin frowned deeply, considering it. But when he looked at Dodger who nodded, then at Pam's eager face, he finally sighed and said, "Okay, but I'm gonna quiz you first after you've studied the books. Only then will you try the real thing. I mean, it's not like you try it once or twice and learn how to fly, it takes time, and training. Got it?"

She nodded. "I got it. Just you wait. I'll be a quick learner. Then we won't have to worry about only having one pilot." Pam's head dropped back down through the skylight and was gone as she descended the ladder.

Dodger patted Kevin on the back. "Well, buddy, it looks like you can be replaced soon."

Kevin smiled halfheartedly, not liking the idea at all. The one thing he brought to the group was being the only pilot. Once Pam learned, that position would be taken away.

"Come on, let's go shoot some more zombies, we're letting Pete have all the fun," Dodger said, and walked back to join Pete.

Kevin paused for a few seconds, thinking, then joined the two troopers at some more target practice.

* * *

"Come on, get up, Kevin," Pam said. "Today's the day you teach me to fly." It had been two weeks since she'd asked Kevin to teach her how to pilot the helicopter. She'd studied every day and after a quiz last night, Kevin had finally agreed it was time to actually have her sit in the pilot's seat.

Kevin groaned in his sleep and rolled over, Pam on the bed beside him. She'd woken early today, and after dressing and washing up, had immediately woken Kevin. Only the man wouldn't get up.

"I'm warning you," she said. "Get up or I'll make you get up."

He moaned some more but refused to wake.

"Okay, you asked for it." She got up on her knees, turned around so her ass was facing his face, and let out the loudest fart imaginable.

Kevin's eyes snapped open an instant later, his nose scrunching up as the fart washed over him. "Christ, what the hell, Pam?" He jumped out of the bed and took a few steps away, the lower half of his face buried in his t-shirt. "God, what the hell have you been eating?"

"Never mind that," she said, tossing his clothes at him. "Just get dressed so you can teach me how to fly."

Mumbling in annoyance the entire time, he did what she said, and after he'd used the bathroom and had a cup of coffee, the same cup still in his hand with a fresh refill, they went up to the roof and climbed into the helicopter, only this time Pam was in the pilot's seat, the controls before her. Kevin went over the instruments again the way he'd been taught, and Pam eagerly listened to everything he said. In a matter of minutes, the helicopter was in the air, hovering ten feet off the roof, Pam the one in control. Pam's face was set in total concentration. Her jaw was taut, her eyes half closed as she tried to avoid the glare of the sun. Kevin, his eyes locked on the instrument panel, coached her along, ever waiting for the moment when he would have to grab the controls from her or risk crashing into the mall.

But that moment never came. Pam was a natural and caught on even easier than Kevin would have imagined. He hated to admit it but she was taking to flying even better than he had when he'd taken his lessons.

In an hour from the second she'd stepped into the cockpit, she had gotten the hang of taking off and landing, and understood the throttle and rudder controls as well. She buzzed round the mall, flying high in a zigzag pattern until finally retuning to the roof.

As the landing skids touched down for the fifth time in an hour, Pam turned to look at Kevin, her eyes wide as she waited for his final answer.

"Shit, Pam, you did it. You did great."

"I did?" she said.

"Yup, you're a natural."

She was so excited by his reply that she leaned over and hugged him, then they kissed. At first it wasn't much, but a second later they were passionately kissing, as above them, the rotor blades began to cycle down.

"Come on, let's go back down inside. I swear, I'm gonna wreck you," Kevin said, breathing heavily. He wanted to fuck her, something he hadn't done in a while. Her tits were bigger now that she was pregnant, and though her belly was bigger, she still had managed to keep her figure. Her ass was a little plumper sure, but it was still curvaceous.

"Okay," was all she said, her face red from passion.

"And maybe we could do anal this time?"

She paused as she was leaving the helicopter, a slight smile on her lips. "Maybe, I'll think about it."

"Yes," he said and pumped a fist as she turned her back on him.

They climbed out of the chopper, one on each side, and with Pam going first down the ladder, quickly followed by Kevin, the two disappeared from the roof to begin their lovemaking in their bed.

But unknown to the couple as they left the roof, three sets of eyes had been on them as the helicopter had flown around the shopping mall.

The names of the three men were Bernie, Bob and Phil. All three of them were middle-aged, with receding hairlines and large noses. They wore little red caps made of felt on their heads with a single red tassel hanging from the top, and they were armed to the teeth. Behind them, three small toy cars, just big enough to hold the men, sat waiting for their owners to return. All three men were armed with an assortment of weapons: guns, knives, and one had a club.

The one named Bernie lowered a pair of Bushnell binoculars and sneered. "Will you look at that," he said, gesturing to the mall a quarter mile away. "Whoever those people are, they got the whole fucking place to themselves."

The man named Bob lowered his own pair of binoculars. "Yeah, and it looks like they got the doors secured, too. They must have taken the place back in the beginning and now they're livin' in style."

"Well, not for long," Bernie added. "By the time we're through with them, they'll be walking around like the rest of the rotters, and that place will be ours."

"How many you think are in there?" the third man asked.

"Beats me, Phil," Bernie replied. "Can't be more than a half dozen or so. If there were more people we would've seen them patrolling the roof, but other than those two in the helicopter there's been no one around. Nah…" He shook his head. "I don't think there's too many in there. We can take them easy."

"But what about all the rotters? How we gonna deal with them?" Bob asked.

"We can take them fast," Bernie explained. "They move so damn slow, we can get in and out before half of them have figured out we're around." He chuckled. "Besides, I've been wanting to try out old Betsy here." He patted a small chainsaw lying beside him.

"When are we gonna go? Now?" Phil asked.

Bernie shook his head. "No, we wait for tomorrow morning, right at sunrise. They'll probably all be sleeping like babies. We'll come right in and take them all by surprise."

"But what if they got people on watch?" Phil asked.

Bernie turned so he was looking right at Phil. "What did I just say, moron? So far we've been watching for hours and there's been no one up there on that roof but the two people in the helicopter. Shit, if it hadn't been for it buzzing the building, we wouldn't have even bothered to stop here, figuring the mall was overrun like the others we've come across."

"Lucky us, huh?" Bob said with an evil grin.

"Yeah, man, lucky for us. But unlucky for whoever's in that shopping mall." Bernie picked up his chainsaw, turned, and walked back to his little car, the others following like loyal puppies. "Let's get back to the others and tell them what we found." He smiled malevolently. "By the time we're through with the people in that shopping mall, they're gonna know the name of Shriners Club 154."

Chapter 14

The first sign that something was wrong in the shopping mall came at a little before five in the morning. It was Pam who'd heard the noise. She'd had to pee, the baby pressing on her bladder.

The sound of the glass breaking on the doors at the north side of the mall wasn't what got her attention, but the sound of gunfire, and the echo of small motors reverberating off the walls of the building.

Without waking the others, Pam went to the door leading to the stairwell, which in turn would bring her down to the first floor of the mall. Taking the steps carefully, as she didn't want to fall and risk her baby—or her neck—she made her way down the stairs, then cracked the fire door leading into the mall. Pam's eyes went wide at what she saw. A dozen or so men, all wearing bright red felt caps with tassels, more than half driving small red cars only slightly big enough to hold them, were running down and rolling along the long hallway, more than a score of zombies at their backs, with even more pouring through the now destroyed glass doors.

The mall had been breached, and it hadn't been the dead that did it, but other humans who had invaded Pam's sanctuary. She didn't bother to ponder why they dressed so oddly, what with their weird hats and little cars. All she saw were the guns and weapons they carried. One man wielded a chainsaw, hacking and slashing at the zombies around him.

She watched in amazement as a zombie approached the man, and he raised the chainsaw and brought it down on the zombie's head, then continued downward, cutting the body in half. When he reached the groin, the zombie's two pieces parted, one to the left and one to the right, peeling apart like taffy stuck to a wall. The internal organs splashed out to spread across the floor, causing three more zombies to slip and trip. Like they were on ice, their feet went out from under them, and they fell hard onto their backs. But the chainsaw-wielding man was there to cut off their heads and limbs. He laughed gleefully as he worked, relishing the carnage.

Others in the group were going into the stores, ransacking them for anything they could grab. In the blink of an eye, Pam's home for months was being invaded and destroyed.

Slamming the door closed in horror and fear, Pam turned and dashed up the stairs, taking two at a time. She made it halfway up before she had to slow down. The baby took a lot out of her and sometimes she forgot she wasn't as nimble as before. Taking the rest of the stairs one at a time, a hand holding her belly, as if that would make her be okay, she reached the landing and the door leading into her and the men's home.

Once inside, she went to Dodger first, waking him and quickly explaining what was happening. He believed her instantly, for while she told him what she'd seen, the faint sound of gunshots filtered into the room from the mall.

"Wake the others," Dodger said. He jumped to his feet and began donning his SWAT uniform. Next came his guns, and lastly his knife. There was a small gun store in the mall as well, and he and the others had made sure to take as much stuff as they could carry back to their living space, where the guns were mounted to the wall on racks or in boxes. He looked up as Kevin and Pete came into the room. "You guys ready?"

"Yeah, but for what?" Pete asked. His mouth was full of some kind of pastry. Dodger didn't say anything; he was used to the fat man eating constantly by now.

"To take back this place," Dodger said.

"But there's too many of them," Pam said. "Why do you have to fight? We can all get into the helicopter and just fly away. Let them have this place, it's not worth dying for."

"Fuck that," Dodger said. "We took this place, made it ours. They don't get the right to come in here and take it from us." He looked at Pete and Kevin. "You with me, guys?"

"Hell yeah," Kevin said, holding a shotgun in his hand. "This is our place now, and goddamn it we'll fight to keep it."

Pete only nodded as he stuffed his mouth full of the remaining pastry. He did give a thumbs-up when the nod wasn't sufficient for the others.

"But there's too many of them. Don't be fools," Pam reasoned. "You don't have to do this. Shit, it's so cliché, too. The rational thing to do would be for us to fly away and let them have this place. We can find someplace just as good."

Dodger walked over to Pam, his nose inches from hers. "Yeah, Pam, we could do that. But in case you forgot, I got a dick between my legs and that means I have to fight for shit, even if it makes no sense at all." He turned and left the room, the other two men right behind him.

Kevin glanced at Pam, shrugging a shoulder and giving her a half-smile. It was his way of telling her sorry, that he was with Dodger and Pete, but that he felt bad for her. After she had learned to fly yesterday, their relationship had been rekindled even more, as if they had seen each other for the first time again. They had screwed and talked long into the night after her successful lesson, and now he was going off to fight, and probably die.

Dodger charged down the stairs and stopped at the fire door leading into the mall. Pete and Kevin were right behind him, though Pete was huffing and puffing, as if the man had run a mile in minutes. Dodger looked at Pete and frowned disapprovingly.

Pete only smiled, which seemed wider because of the sugar on his face from his devoured pastry.

"Wipe your damn mouth at least," Dodger whispered. "You look stupid."

Pete put on an embarrassed look and wiped his mouth and chin with his sleeve. Wearing his SWAT inform as well, the sugar stood out brightly on the black material. The uniform was tighter than it was before, too, and some of the buttons looked about ready to burst free at any moment.

Dodger cracked the door and peered into the mall hallway, frowning deeply at what he saw.

This is why he had said they should live in the offices off the main track of the mall. Sure they could have set up house in one of the department stores, with all the furniture there to simply move around, and not lug up the stairs to the offices. But if they had been living in the mall now, there would have been no escape, no warning of the raiders arrival until it was too late to do anything.

The Shriners zipped by the door, not noticing it was cracked, and soon most of them were far down the hallway, in search of booty.

"Okay, it's clear. Pete, you go to the left, Kevin, you're with me. Take out as many of the assholes as you can, and once they're either dead or on the run, we can figure out how to secure the glass doors they broke."

"Got it," Pete said.

The three men charged into the hallway, their guns leveled and aimed at whatever they might find. That happened to be a trio of zombies and one of the Shriners, who was late to the party.

The man let go of the tiny steering wheel of the car he was in so he could use both hands to fire the rifle he carried, but Dodger and Pete were faster. Before the man could pull the trigger on the rifle, he was riddled with bullets, along with the three zombies around him. All four bodies were prone on the floor a second later, the little car rolling to the side, now devoid of a driver.

Dodger studied the little red car, his head cocking to the side. "What the fuck?" was all he could think to say.

"That looks like a Shriner's toy car," Kevin said. "They ride them in parades."

"Shriners?" Pete asked. "Who the fuck are they?"

"Well," Kevin explained, "they're a Masonic club. They like to help children, too. You'd see them in holiday parades a lot of the time."

"Maybe before," Dodger said. "But these bunch of assholes are out for themselves. Come on, let's move out. The longer we wait the more they're gonna destroy our mall."

As the three men moved out, more and more zombies poured into the shopping mall via the now destroyed glass doors. In the midst of the crowd of undead were a few Shriners, those that had been overly confident and had ended up becoming fodder for the dead. Now, they too, wandered into the shopping mall, only now they were fighting for the other team than the one they'd begun with that morning.

As the Shriners went deeper into the mall; they whooped and clapped at all the wonderful items on display. Quickly they began gathering whatever they could. Some on the cars pulled little wagons and these were soon filled high with clothes, electronics and both canned and dried food.

"Holy shit, man," Bob said to Bernie. "This place is a gold mine."

"See, didn't I tell you it would be?" Bernie replied, his arms full of loot.

Gunshots suddenly rang out and both Bernie and Bob dropped what they were carrying, turning to see two men, one all in black, running at them, firing while they ran.

"Who the fuck are they?" Bob yelled.

"Must be the people living here, they've come to take back what's ours now." Bernie raised his gun and fired. "And we're gonna keep it, too!" He gestured to a few Shriners around him to get their attention, the men not realizing they were being shot at in all the chaos—gunshots sounded sporadically all the time as the Shriners took out the zombies threatening them. "Don't just stand there, you idiots, shoot those guys!"

The other Shriners stopped what they were doing and pulled their guns, then began to fire at Kevin and Dodger, both men dashing to the side to take cover behind a large stone planter. The tree within it was plastic, and dust rained down on the men as Dodger bumped the planter in his haste to find protection. Bullets whined past him and Kevin, only a few even coming close to hitting them.

Pete was also in an ongoing battle with a group of five Shriners, all with automatic machine guns. Pinned down behind a bagel kiosk, Pete fired back at his attackers, but to no avail. They had him trapped. Figuring if he was stuck he might as well eat, he reached up and grabbed a very old bagel from the kiosk, biting into the brittle dough. It hadn't molded, but had turned as hard a rock. Chewing on the piece he carved off with his teeth, he forced the mouthful down and went in for more, all the while shooting at his attackers.

Then he got lucky and one of the Shriners popped his head out a little too far from behind his hiding place. Pete shot the man in the face, the visage disappearing in a spray of blood and brain matter, the back of the man's head disintegrating as the bullet exited his skull. The body dropped to the floor and lay still, blood squirting out of the jagged, open wound.

Feeling proud of his marksmanship, Pete prepared to shoot another Shriner that was poking his head up from around the bench he was hiding behind, when suddenly Pete felt hands grab his arms and shoulders.

"What the fu…" he began around a mouthful of bagel, but never finished his sentence when he turned to find that four zombies had snuck up on him unawares, his attention focused forward, at the gunmen.

Pete tried to get up, to swing the rifle around to shoot the zombies, but as he stood up, one of the Shriners took the opportunity to have such a large target in view and fired his gun, catching Pete in the side. The bullet went in like a knife, then struck a rib and rebounded back out Pete's front. The fat man's mouth dropped open as searing pain filled him from head to toe. The hesitation he had upon being shot was all the zombies needed to press their attack. Pete was forced to the floor, where teeth and sharp fingernails began to tear at his clothes, to reach the dark flesh beneath.

Long, greasy entrails were ripped from Pete's abdomen as the man's eyes bulged from their sockets, and rolls of fat, yellow and resembling cottage cheese, spilled out onto the floor. His mouth opened and closed but nothing came out, blood shooting out from between his lips, as his insides were fed on before his eyes. His stomach was torn open, exposing the large breakfast he'd had before leaving the offices, where even now Pam waited, scared and wondering how the men were faring.

Pete felt his ribs cracked open as multiple hands tore at his ribcage, and then the beating heart within. His could only stare in abject amazement as his heart was plucked from his chest, the ventricles still squirting warm blood across his face. A zombie sank its teeth into the still-pulsing muscle, tearing at the tough meat with its yellowed teeth. That was the last thing Pete saw before death took him, his eyes fluttering, the orbs rolling back into his head, just before multiple fingers scooped them out to chomp down on the soft and squishy morsels.

While the zombies fed, the remaining Shriners who had been pinned down, hopped back onto their little red cars and drove past Pete, honking and laughing as they passed him.

Pete however, was already gone, and didn't hear any of the taunting.

Pam could hear the gun battle raging outside in the mall and it made her sick to her stomach. Were the men all right? They must be or the gunshots wouldn't be so loud and coming so fast. But then again, the people with the red hats could be just shooting zombies, and the men she knew and loved could already be dead.

She looked back into the room and the skylight from where she stood at the door leading into the stairwell. All she had to do was climb the ladder and get into the helicopter, and a few minutes later she could fly away.

This would be a last ditch effort on her part, and only if the men didn't return. If even one of them came back, her escape option would only be delayed, then they could leave together. Though she wanted all of them to return, if she had to choose, Kevin was her first choice.

She cared for Dodger and Pete deeply, but Kevin was the man she loved, and so was her only choice if it came right down to it. She sent out a prayer into the void that he was safe, and would return to her shortly.

She tried not to think of what would happen if none of them returned. She was strong, yes, but not strong enough to survive alone in the world the way it was now, and not with a baby due.

Thoughts of being out in the world alone made her cringe, filling her with dread. Once more she sent out good thoughts that the others would be victorious and return to her, for the alternative was too dire to contemplate.

Kevin's heart skipped a beat or two, as he found himself trapped by the Shriners on one side and the zombies on the other.

He and Dodger had separated a minute ago when a group of Shriners and zombies had attacked them simultaneously. The Shriners were also beleaguered on two fronts. Their careless entrance into the shopping mall now had them fighting the three living defenders of the mall, and with the zombies, which wanted nothing more than to feed on either party of humans. Good or bad, none of it mattered to them, only the warm meat of the humans.

Kevin ducked behind a mannequin as bullets zipped by his head. He swallowed the knot in his throat and forced the fear within him back down. This was the time he'd been training for with Dodger. This was what it meant to be a man. To fight for what was yours. He knew how to shoot; now he had to take that learning and use it to defend the shopping mall.

The zombies moaned behind him and he shot at the closest one, hitting it in the neck. The zombie spun around like it was a top, but soon righted itself and continued walking towards Kevin, the others right behind it.

"Come on, man!" one of the Shriners called out to Kevin. "Don't make this hard on yourself. Just stand up so we can see you and we'll make it quick. Don't and we'll make you suffer, then feed you to the rotters."

Kevin's reply was to shoot at the man, only the Shriner ducked back and the bullet missed. Kevin spun around as the zombies came ever closer. He had seconds now before he had to either run or fight, and he knew there were too many zombies to fight.

Thinking about what Dodger would do, he decided to just go for it, and he burst from his hiding spot, trying to make it across the aisle of the department store he was in. But the Shriners were ready for him and a barrage of bullets flew his way. One struck him in the arm but it was only a flesh wound, but then one hit his left thigh, making him fall to the floor while yelling out in pain.

The Shriners laughed and came out of hiding, but then saw the zombies shuffling forward and turned and walked away, one of the men saying, "Leave him for the rotters. With that leg he won't get far."

Kevin tried to crawl away, but with both his arm and leg shot, he could barely manage to move. He rolled onto his back as the zombie shuffled forward. He saw that a few of the zombies were fresh ones, and that they wore the red felt hats of the same group of men he'd been fighting only moments ago. The Shriners were taking heavy casualties it seemed as well, and Kevin smiled at that. Though he had lost, he knew Dodger would survive, and that he would make sure Pam was safe.

As the zombies fell on Kevin and he fought them off, shooting them as fast as they came at him, Kevin's smile never wavered, even when one of the newly dead Shriner-zombies sank its teeth into his throat, tearing it out, the felt hat falling on top of Kevin's chest. Kevin fired again and again, killing all the zombies, but as the last one fell with a bullet to the head, Kevin bled out and lost consciousness, falling into death—his last thought was of Pam, and how he needed to return to her.

But in the new world, death wasn't the end, and as there were no zombies around to feed on Kevin's corpse, he soon revived. Kevin sat up, saw the felt hat that had fallen into his lap and picked it up. He put it on, moving the tassel away from his face, then slowly, he stood up. The last thought before death had been about Pam, and now, even in death, that thought remained. Slowly and with great patience, he began to walk down the aisle of the department store, then into the hallway. His gait was awkward thanks to his leg wound, and that leg was stiff and barely working. He turned in the direction of the offices, and Pam, who was still waiting for Kevin's return.

As Kevin walked, his face already having taken on a pale visage, his eyes blank and staring, blood seeping from the wound in his throat, Pam had no way of knowing that Kevin was still going to return to her, only now as a zombie.

More zombies joined Kevin as he walked through the mall, as if they somehow sensed that this particular zombie knew where it was going, and that at the end of its journey there would be food.

All around the mall, the Shriners were being torn apart, the sheer number of the dead finally overwhelming them. Bernie lay in the center of the mall, his chainsaw a few feet away, as more than a dozen zombies fought for the opportunity to tear him apart. Another group of zombies surrounded Phil, their arms and hands working as they ripped into him, Phil screaming loudly. But then the screams stopped abruptly and one zombie moved away from the crowd, Phil's severed head in its hands.

The zombie slid a hand into Phil's open neck and dug deep into the skull. Pulling out a heaping portion of brains, it shoved them into its mouth, the slushy goop squirting around its lips to splatter onto the floor. But other zombies were there to slurp up the sloppy seconds.

Bob was long gone, his body parts scattered to more than a dozen zombies, who had then wandered off to feed in peace. Those few Shriners that managed to escape the mall were quickly overwhelmed outside in the parking lot, their little cars no match for all the swarming bodies. They all died screaming and in great pain, suffering to the last second before death took them, and only a very few managed to revive to join the walking dead; most were devoured, torn apart until there was nothing left to revive.

Dodger ran through the shopping mall, shooting zombies when they blocked his path, avoiding others when it was possible. The dead were everywhere, filling every hallway, every corridor and store. There would be no way to salvage what had happened; the mall was lost. The only thing left to do was escape.

But escape to where? The simple fact that the Shriners had showed up and had attacked meant that civilization had broken down for good and it wasn't going to be recovering anytime soon, if ever.

There was nowhere to go, and he knew that, though he didn't want to accept it. Sure, they had the helicopter, but it was terribly low on fuel, barely enough to make it a few miles. As Dodger ran, he hoped Kevin had made it back to the offices, for since the man had been separated from Dodger, the trooper hadn't seen or heard from him. For all Dodger knew, Kevin was dead.

No sooner did Dodger think about where Pete was, wondering how the fat trooper was doing, than he ran past the large mess that was Pete's corpse. Or what was left of it. The fat man was more bones and blood than anything else, only the SWAT uniform a way for Dodger to identify his fallen friend. Cursing loudly, he shot the seven zombies feeding on Pete's corpse, then began running again, wanting to reach Pam, and hopefully, Kevin as well.

As he ran he could smell smoke, and now that he really looked, he could see there was a cloudiness to the air. It seemed to be coming from the hallway that led to the video store.

Unknown to Dodger, a few of the zombies had gotten into the store and had knocked over the gas can next to the generator used to run a TV and VCR so the men could watch porn. The spilled gas wasn't an issue, but then another zombie knocked over a table set up near the generator, a screwdriver on the table falling into the gas, where it created a spark as it rebounded off the floor. It was enough to ignite the gas, and soon a raging inferno was blossoming, one that threatened to consume the entire shopping mall.

Forcing back the urge to cough, Dodger did his best to breathe through his nose as he made his way back to Pam. Racing up the stairs leading to the office space, he burst through the door in time to see Pam swinging around with a rifle in her hands. "Wait, it's me, don't shoot!" Dodger yelled, his hands up before him.

Pam lowered the rifle, relief on her face as she went to him. "Kevin, is he with you?" she asked hopefully.

"I thought he'd be here, waiting with you. He's not back yet?" he asked.

She shook her head. "No, I hope he's okay."

"Maybe he's just pinned down is all. Most of the Shriners are either dead or retreating, we can get Kevin then."

Pam realized Pete wasn't with Dodger and she asked, "Where's Pete?"

Dodger opened his mouth to reply and then closed it, his head lowering as he shook it sadly.

"Oh no," was all Pam could say. Then she added with a shrug, "At least we'll get better gas mileage in the helicopter with him gone."

"Yeah, his fat ass must have been a hell of a workout for the engine. I'm gonna miss him," Dodger added.

There was noise coming from the stairwell and both of them turned as one to the door.

"Could it be Kevin?" she asked. Pam began moving towards the door but Dodger grabbed her arm. "No, wait, it might be him, and it might not be."

"What do you mean?" she asked, not understanding.

"Just wait," he said, his handgun gripped tightly in his right hand, his rifle slung over his shoulder.

The sound of many feet echoing in the stairwell filtered through the door and Dodger grabbed Pam and shoved her gently towards the ladder, where she had put some bags on the floor in case they needed to make a quick getaway.

"You need to go," he said coldly. "Whoever's in the stairwell can't be a friend. If Kevin's with them then that means he's a zombie."

"No," she said. "He can't be." She had tears in her eyes as she glared at Dodger. "He can't be one of them."

"He sure as shit can. Now stop talking and go. You have a baby to take care of once you give birth. Go, I'll keep them from following you."

"But what about Kevin?"

"I'll deal with Kevin," he said flatly. "Now go!" he yelled, shoving her a little harder.

She didn't want to go but she also knew for her to ascend the ladder it took a few seconds longer than it used to. "Okay, but you're coming right behind me, right?"

Dodger turned to face her, as the sounds outside the door grew ever louder. Only seconds remained. "No, I don't want to go with you."

"You what? What the fuck are you talking about?"

"You heard me," he replied. "There's nothing left for me out there, and it just feels like I'm rehashing a story everyone knows about, a plot that's been done to death over and over again. Besides, if it's just you in the chopper, you'll get better distance with the remaining fuel if there's less weight to carry. Maybe you'll be able to reach safety before you run out of gas."

"But..."

"No buts, damn it, just go!"

"No, Dodger, not without you!" She wasn't going to leave without him. Not just because she didn't want to see him die, but because she didn't want to fly away alone, out there, where she would be helpless, what with the baby and all. Sure, she could shoot, but what would she do when she ran out of bullets?

She was snapped back to reality as the door leading to the stairwell was kicked open and in came a crowd of zombies, Kevin in the lead.

"Shit," Dodger said. "Now that I think of it, I really should have locked that door when I came in here." He shrugged. "Oh well, live and learn." He raised his gun and shot Kevin in the head, blowing out the back of his skull, Kevin's brains splattering the wall behind him.

The rest of the zombies swarmed around his fallen body, lunging for Dodger, who forced Pam to the ladder as he held off the attacking zombies. "Go, there's no more time!"

Pam did as she was told, terrified as the attacking zombies came for her. She rushed up the ladder, a few trying to grab her feet but missing. Dodger shot at them, yelling at them to get their attention, as he led the zombies into the next room. Most followed, but a few began to climb the ladder clumsily.

Dodger holstered his revolver when he fired the last bullet, and he began to use his rifle, shooting the zombies one at a time until the magazine ran dry. Throwing the rifle at one of the zombies, he pulled a smaller handgun from a holster hanging by his side. The gun held six bullets and he began to fire at the zombies. But he could only use five bullets on the zombies—he needed one for himself.

He fired again and again, until he had that one remaining bullet. He placed it to his temple as the zombies surrounded him.

As he pressed the muzzle to his temple, feeling the hot metal burn his skin, his mind flashed to Pam, who even now would be waiting anxiously at the helicopter, hoping he would somehow change his mind and go with her.

But she would be wrong. He'd had enough, and though it was the coward's way out, it was the death of his choosing, which was more than a lot of people could say had been their exit from this life. Besides, the idea of dealing with Pam and a screaming baby wasn't a future he would enjoy. Truth be told, he hated kids, the little brats, always crying and whining, their noses running, full of germs and wise-ass responses.

As the zombies closed in, their hands reaching for him, tearing at his uniform, he closed his eyes and let out the breath he was holding.

"Well, fellas, it's been a fucking blast, see you in the funny papers."

He squeezed the trigger.

Pam stood at the helicopter, her right foot on the landing skid, her left one on the mall roof.

The rotor blades were spinning fast, as she had taken a few seconds to get the engine warmed up. All she had to do was hop into the pilot's seat, and an instant later the helicopter would be flying away, leaving the shopping mall to the zombies.

Smoke could be seen from multiple places on the long and wide roof, and she knew the mall was burning.

Even as she watched, sections of the roof fell in as the inferno fed on itself, sucking in more oxygen with each passing second.

There was no doubt all was lost at the shopping mall, and now that Pam looked back to when they'd first arrived, she wondered why she'd let the men talk her into staying.

The gunshots within the office rooms that had been filtering out of the open skylight suddenly ceased, and a second later the first zombie appeared, climbing out of the skylight and onto the roof.

More were behind it, and soon a dozen were shambling towards Pam. Still she waited, hoping beyond hope that Dodger would appear, fighting his way through the zombies like a quarterback going for the touchdown. But when a single gunshot sounded, she felt herself jump, the shot fatal in its singularity.

The zombies moved closer, and still Pam waited, but when the first zombie was only ten feet away, Pam realized that Dodger wasn't coming, and what that lone gunshot truly meant.

She looked at the helicopter and the bags piled within it, then down at her belly, where new life was even now growing.

But she didn't like her odds, and the idea of fleeing the mall alone filled her with far too much terror for her liking.

No, better to end it quick.

Before she could change her mind, she yelled, "Fuck you all!" to the zombies, then she stepped up on the highest part of the landing skid, and thrust her head up into the spinning rotor blades.

She never felt a thing, the blades slicing her head in half, just above her nose. The top of her skull flew across the roof and bounced once before landing at the feet of a zombie, who picked it up and began scooping out hearty handfuls of brains, as the long hair blew in the wind.

Pam's body tumbled to the rooftop, the rest of her brains spilling onto the gravel-covered roof, her arms and legs twitching, despite her already being dead.

The zombies surrounded the body, and quickly began tearing at it. Soon Pam was a bloody mess of body parts, and one zombie, pushing through the pack, was seen to be carrying what looked like a small and bloody doll. As it walked, it ripped off and then shoved the little limbs into its mouth, chewing happily, the object looking like red taffy as the zombie pulled it apart with its teeth.

One adventurous zombie climbed into the helicopter, and without understanding what it was doing, pushed on the throttle, making the helicopter jump into the air before skewing sideways.

The rotor blades sliced into the roof before breaking apart, some of the pieces of the blades flying horizontally and cutting zombies in two at the waist.

The upper parts of the zombies fell over and then began to crawl with the use of their arms and hands, while the bottom portions were left behind.

The rotors gone, and a piece hitting the engine and severing the fuel line, the helicopter erupted into a raging fireball that consumed the entire section of roof it was on.

The flames spread quickly, meshing with the already raging inferno, until the flames reached fifty feet into the sky.

Every zombie on the roof was consumed in the red hot blaze, the bodies twitching and glowing like red hot ash. Mouths went slack as eyeballs popped, skin melting as if the zombies were made of wax.

The funeral pyre was all encompassing, a cleansing of the shopping mall that had been long in coming, and though deadly, in many ways it was beautiful. The reds and oranges flickered and glowed, while the rising sun kissed the sky on a new day.

Nothing alive was in the area to see the shopping mall burn, though the remaining zombies in the parking lot of the mall all turned to stare, as if hypnotized by the growing fireball.

From miles around, every zombie that could see the smoke began to walk in that direction, as if the fire was a signal, a siren calling out to them to come.

One single ash floated on the wind, rising higher and higher into the sky, until finally, it melted into the welcoming rays of a new dawn.

A dawn filled with the walking dead.

Life is a comedy for those who think and a tragedy for those who feel.

Jean de la Bruyere
1645-1696

THE PLACE TO GO FOR ZOMBIE AND APOCALYPTIC FICTION

LIVING DEAD PRESS

WHERE THE DEAD WALK

www.livingdeadpress.com

ZOMBIES, MONSTERS, CREATURES OF THE NIGHT
OPEN CASKET PRESS
OPEN CASKET PRESS.COM
THE NEW NAME IN HORROR

VICTORY OF THE DEAD
ANTHONY GIANGREGORIO

STFU PUBLISHING.COM
FOR HORROR THAT DOESN'T HOLD BACK

www.ingramcontent.com/pod-product-compliance
Lightning Source LLC
Chambersburg PA
CBHW070504120726
47910CB00003B/1120